The Enigma of Heston Grange

The sequel to The Cryptic Lines

Richard Storry

By the same author

The Cryptic Lines
Order of Merit
The Black Talisman
The Virtual Lives of Godfrey Plunkett

The Ruritanian Rogues Saga:
Volume I: A Looming of Vultures
Volume II: A Nest of Vipers
Volume III: A Shroud of Darkness
Volume IV: A Betrayal of Trust
Volume V: A Hoard of Treasures
Volume VI: A Conflict of Loyalties

Cover design: Gergö Pocsai

All titles are available from www.crypticpublications.com in paperback, in audio format and as downloads for e-readers.

ISBN: 9798634553177

Dear Reader,

Welcome to my latest mysterious tale! I imagine that many of you will already have read the prequel to this volume, entitled *The Cryptic Lines*. If so, you will be well placed to make the most of what the following pages contain. However, for anyone who has not read the earlier book, whilst I believe that this new tale can stand alone in its own right, I would urge you to acquaint yourself with the previous story, in order to maximise your understanding and enjoyment.

And now I'll get out of the way, and simply say...

Welcome (back) to Heston Grange!

Best wishes,

R.S.
London, March, 2020

The Enigma of Heston Grange

The enigma I will not explain –
its dark saying must be left unguessed
—Sir Edward Elgar

CHAPTER 1

Carrying a silver salver, upon which lay a small cream coloured envelope, the elderly butler moved slowly across the cavernous entrance hall.

In years gone by, the sound of his swift footsteps would have echoed and reverberated around the spacious foyer, as what would then have been firm leather soles clipped sharply against the smooth polished surface of the flagstone floor.

These days, though, his less-than-agile feet barely left the floor as he moved. Instead, his now soft-soled footwear produced a quiet, muffled sound, as he shuffled his way across the hall in answer to the summons from his master, who awaited him by the fire in his study. Naturally, the butler already knew the purpose of his being called – since it was always the same at this time of the evening. Consequently, the tray which he was bearing was occupied not just by the envelope only, but also by an ornate china pot of chamomile tea, together with some freshly baked biscuits, still warm from the oven.

Outside, while it was not yet late, the evening was already dark and the wind was howling. It whistled and screeched as it searched for, and often found, every nook and cranny of the rambling old mansion. Some of the older window frames found themselves unable to keep out the ever-invading draughts while, at the same time, strips of ancient guttering which had gradually loosened over the years now rattled against the eaves, straining against the ageing nails, which did their valiant best to hold them in place.

As he journeyed across the hallway, the old servant paused for a moment when he heard an ominous scraping, followed a moment later by the sound of something smashing. The noise had come from the porch which overhung the large front door.

The butler rolled his eyes.

The ferocious wind had managed to dislodge yet another of the roof tiles which, he knew, he would find lying outside the door in the morning, in a mass of broken fragments.

A look of sadness crossed the aged face.

He was old enough to be able to recall the time when Heston Grange had stood proud, imposing and resplendent. In those days, there was not a thing out of place, the stonework was well defined, and the only creaking to be heard was the pleasantly re-assuring sound caused by someone traversing one of the many wooden-floored landings.

Now, though, things were very different.

As the nearby ocean had continued its unending onslaught on the soft stone forming the cliffs upon which the crumbling mansion perched, the once magnificent dwelling was, little by little, being brought closer and yet perilously closer to the edge.

At first, the owner, Charles Seymour, having inherited the vast house from his father, had all manner of ambitious and exciting plans for it. These included refurbishing the west wing, bringing in period furniture and artwork, and turning part of it into a museum. It had been his intention to have the gardens tidied up and opened to the public; and some of the outbuildings would have been perfect for conversion, making ideal studios for local craftsmen to come and demonstrate their skills, such as carving and fashioning pottery, and making their creations available for sale. Charles had also wanted to transform the stables into a small zoo for baby farm animals, which children from nearby schools could come and visit. All of this would have been in addition to his numerous contributions to community life: unlike his father, Charles was definitely not a recluse, preferring instead to be actively involved in all manner of local activities and events. If anything, he had become something of a local celebrity. He was always being recognised when he ventured into the nearest town, to the point that even outings which should have taken just a few minutes would often take much longer, as he found himself being engaged in any number of conversations with locals whom he happened to meet as he walked along the high street.

His plans for the house, however, were thwarted by none other than Mother Nature herself. She continued to insist on having her way, by refusing to cease her relentless erosion of the cliff face. Charles had sought expert advice and had been told that whilst it was not certain, it was nevertheless distinctly possible that the house would gradually be brought nearer and nearer to the edge of the cliffs, with the violent waves beneath. Consequently, and with great reluctance, Charles had realised that there was little point in continuing with his plans any further. Even the insurance company had noted this; whilst they had not actually refused to renew the insurance, the premium had been raised to such a stratospheric level that it had become ridiculous. This was a source of deep disappointment to both himself and the servants: his loyal butler, James, and the indefatigable housekeeper, Mrs Gillcarey, both of whom had worked at the house for many decades. It was with great heaviness of heart that they had finally come to recognise, and reluctantly accept the real possibility, that the great house may well, at some point in the future, simply crumble away into the sea.

But not quite yet.

Hopefully, there would still be a fair bit of time before then, if, indeed, it were to happen at all. That, at least, was something to be thankful for – for the time being, at any rate.

James had now crossed the hallway and was making his way along one of the many corridors which twisted and turned through the ancient dwelling.

At length, he reached the oak panelled entrance to his master's study and, after balancing the tray expertly on one hand, raised the other to knock politely on the door.

***

Since the momentous day when Charles Seymour, to his complete surprise, had discovered that he was to be the new owner of this sizeable residence, Heston Grange had fascinated him. After hearing revelations from his father, the late Lord Alfred Willoughby, regarding the network of hidden passageways with which the house was riddled, it had become his passion to discover the whereabouts of each one. Some of these he had already happened upon during his earlier search for a large blue sapphire, as part of a frustratingly complex treasure hunt which had been set in motion by his devious parent. Yet there were others too; before his death his father had shown him a good number of them, and their ingeniously concealed entrances were a constant source of fascination for Charles.

However, Lord Alfred had freely admitted his belief that there were a great many others, of which even he was unaware. What was even more tantalising, though, was when the ageing Lord had added, with a mischievous glint in his elderly eye, that there was one passageway in particular which he *did* know about, but which would, in his opinion, be better left undisturbed. This statement drew Charles in like a bee to a honeypot and presented him with a real enigma. Yet, despite all his pleadings, Lord Alfred adamantly refused to disclose its whereabouts. Instead, all he would do was tease, and say that all would become clear in time. And now, with years having elapsed since his Lordship's departure, this mysterious passage remained undiscovered. Where could it possibly be? And what did it conceal which was so important that it would be better to stay away from it? The current owner of this crumbling mansion simply *had* to know, yet desire alone was not sufficient, as Charles knew only too well.

With the passage of time, every so often Charles would chance upon yet another disguised corridor, and feel a now familiar tingle of excitement as he did so. So far, though, none of his discoveries had yielded the hoped for enigma to which Lord Alfred had alluded. Of course, it was always a thrilling moment when a new secret door, passage or partition was revealed, yet so far none of them had contained anything deserving of Lord Alfred's suggestion that it would be better to leave it well alone.

It was always of particular interest to Charles whenever some previously hidden thoroughfare was discovered which led away from the house itself. He had already identified two secret doorways, connecting Heston Grange to the network of tunnels which had been used by smugglers in centuries gone by, and which threaded their way through the soft-chalk cliffs. However, so extensive were these underground passageways that much of this labyrinthine arrangement still remained largely unexplored. The numerous subterranean chambers which were linked by these tunnels would, at one time, have contained huge stashes of illegal contraband, such as bottles rum and casks of whisky, as well as jewels, pistols and gunpowder, and even tea and lace.

However, for all the excitement which would inevitably accompany the discovery of a new passageway, Charles feared he could never be certain that he had found them all – and, all the while, Lord Alfred's final enigma remained, irritatingly, just out of reach.

Seated at the desk in his study, and with the flickering fire in the hearth in need of some extra fuel, Charles was startled by a sudden, tumultuous clap of thunder which rattled the frame of his window and caused a shower of sooty particles to dislodge themselves from the inside of the flue and rain down onto the hot embers below.

Pausing in his work, he looked up and gazed into the glowing coals. The atmosphere inside this pleasant, warm room brought with it a cosy feeling of security and re-assurance, contrasting dramatically with the maelstrom taking place outside, just beyond the latticed window. The storm seemed to be getting worse, and it caused Charles to recall the night, now many years ago, when he had been summoned to assist Lord Alfred with the re-writing of his Will. That simple request had triggered a whole series of events, which had ultimately led to Charles becoming the sole owner of Heston Grange – a fact which, to this day, still astounded him.

The sound of another thunderbolt caused the lights to flicker momentarily, and almost obscured the quiet sound of a polite knock at the door. Charles endeavoured to raise his voice above the sound of the violent weather.

"Come in," he called.

The door opened, and James entered, bearing the tray, together with its contents.

"Good evening, sir."

James crossed the room and set down the tray on a coffee table near to the hearth, which was virtually surrounded by an assortment of comfortable leather-upholstered chairs. Without waiting to be asked, he placed a silver tea strainer across the top of the china cup and began to pour. The sound of the hot beverage tumbling into the waiting receptacle added further to the atmosphere in the room, which was both cheerful and soothing in equal measure.

"It sounds as though this storm will be with us until well into the night," suggested Charles.

"I fear you may be right, sir."

The old butler was about to withdraw when Charles noticed the cream coloured envelope on the tray, and picked it up.

"What's this?" he asked.

"I have no idea, sir. The daily postal delivery already arrived several hours ago. This one has no stamp, and no address – it simply shows your name – so it must have been delivered by hand. It didn't even come through the regular letter box; I found it on the mat by the tradesman's entrance."

With a slight look of puzzlement crossing his forehead, Charles turned it over in his hands. The texture of the paper indicated that it was clearly of good quality.

"Hmm," he said, "Most intriguing. You didn't happen to see who delivered it?"

"I'm afraid I did not, sir, though even if I had, that may not necessarily have thrown any light on the identity of the sender."

"Very true."

James shuffled across the room and began to stoke the

fire, stirring the glowing hot coals with the poker before adding another log which was quickly set ablaze.

"Will that be all, sir?"

"Yes. Thank you, James."

"Then I will bid you goodnight, sir."

A few moments later, the sound of a soft click signalled that the door had closed and that Charles was alone once again.

Silhouetted against the now blazing fire, Charles still held the unopened envelope. What did this mysterious wallet contain? There was only one way to find out. So why didn't he open it? He wasn't quite sure what was causing him to hesitate, yet some deep instinct or perhaps some kind of sixth sense was giving him pause.

The envelope appeared innocent enough. It was perfectly normal, and his name was typed neatly on the front. So what was troubling him?

He waited a moment longer, then reached for the ornate paper knife on his desk. Carefully, he sliced the envelope open and reached inside. What it contained turned out to be a single sheet of paper, folded in half with a well-defined crease. He placed the now empty envelope and paper knife to one side, and slowly unfolded the paper.

His face went suddenly pale.

The message on the paper was very short – only four words, in fact.

With the thunder and lightning outside increasing in ferocity, Charles read and re-read the words. Like his name on the envelope, the words of the message within had also been typed – this communication contained no actual handwriting whatsoever.

At length, Charles allowed his hand to fall to his lap, the message still held between his fingers. Had there been anyone else present in the room, the words would now have been visible to all.

The message read: *We know your secret.*

CHAPTER 2

If the weather was bad, they were not allowed to go out; the best they could hope for was a couple of hours in the recreation room, whose facilities were basic, and which was not really satisfactory.

However, when the weather was fine, they were allowed to exercise for two hours in the quadrangle.

So, on good days, after being escorted in groups from their cells, the inmates would then trudge around in the high-walled courtyard, whilst at all times being under the watchful eye of two guards on duty in the top of the observation tower.

The area was completely enclosed – there was no view of the outside world whatsoever. The bleak, featureless grey walls were high, and topped with shining razor wire.

Some of the prisoners would endeavour to make the most of the opportunity and jog around the perimeter, while others did push-ups and squats. Still others would congregate in small groups and simply chat, savouring the rare opportunity for communication with other human beings in the open air.

One of the inmates was a thick-set, surly character, known by the rest of the prisoners as The Boss. Tall and very strong, he was built like a tank. He was serving a lengthy sentence for causing grievous bodily harm, and appeared to be quite proud of the fact. Not someone to meddle with, he could frequently be seen speaking softly to other prisoners in quiet corners, and even prison guards, striking deals and gaining influence. While most inmates tended to avoid him, he would often make it his business to come and talk to them, and they knew better than to refuse to speak with him.

On this occasion, he came sauntering across to where a group of three other prisoners were talking on the far side of the courtyard. As he approached, to say that the three, who were leaning against the wall with arms folded, snapped to attention, would have been an exaggeration. However, the respect which his arrival commanded was unmistakeable.

"Afternoon, fellas."

"Afternoon, Boss."

The Boss was not one to waste precious time with small-talk and came straight to the point.

"I hear you're going in front of the Parole Board tomorrow?"

The man to whom he spoke nodded, a little nervously. He knew the Boss would not just be chatting to pass the time of day. What was this about? He waited to hear what would be said next.

"At first, it seemed unlikely that you stood any chance with them at all. Now, though, they're probably gonna let you out."

"I'm hoping so – but please don't think that's just 'cos I want to get away from you, Boss."

The man laughed, trying to assert himself and convey a feeling of confidence.

It didn't work.

"What I mean," said the Boss, "is… I *know* they're gonna let you out."

"Really? I hope you're right, Boss, but how can you be so certain?"

The Boss winked.

"Favours," he said.

"Favours?"

"Sure. I give them some information, then they do something for me – that's how it works. You must be aware of that?"

"Well, yes, but –"

"But what?"

The man swallowed. His Adam's apple moved in his throat, and the Boss noticed.

"But… I mean… well… are you saying that my parole hearing will be successful because of something you have told them?"

The Boss nodded.

"Who's the bright penny?" he smirked. "I'll admit it was quite a tough negotiation but, in the end, I managed to persuade them to see the situation from my point of view."

"I appreciate it, Boss, but why would you do that for me?"

The Boss fixed the nervous man with a piercing glare and regarded him with a wry smile. There was a long pause.

"Nothing personal, boys," said the Boss. He was now addressing the two other inmates who were standing there, though his firm gaze never left the first man, "but I need to have a quiet word in private with my friend, here. Would you excuse us?"

They looked a little uncomfortable, as they nodded, then glanced at each other and removed themselves, both quietly relieved to have been given the opportunity.

The Boss waited until they were a sufficient distance away. As a precaution, he then directed a sharp glance towards the guards in the tower, who obligingly turned in the other direction. Finally satisfied, he now spoke again.

"Before we proceed," he said, "it's important you understand that this favour I have done for you could easily be reversed again, just as quickly. You got that?"

"Sure, Boss. Of course. No problem."

"Good answer. That's a good answer."

There was a lengthy silence, which felt increasingly awkward and uncomfortable until the Boss finally spoke again.

"You've been quite a dark horse, haven't you?" he whispered.

A nervous chuckle.

"What do you mean, Boss?"

"Now then, don't play the innocent. You should know me well enough by now to be aware that I don't appreciate game-playing."

"Of course not, Boss. No offence."

"None taken." Both the tone of the reply and the expression on the Boss's face were impassive. "So, let me come to the point. I've heard on the grapevine that you're well connected."

"Well connected, Boss?"

Without warning, the Boss suddenly stepped much closer, invading the man's personal space. "Did you hear what I just said about game playing?" he snarled.

The man gulped, and nodded.

"Do I actually need to tell you who you are related to?"

"No, Boss, of course not."

"Good. So we understand each other then?"

The man nodded again. He had begun to tremble, but was trying to control it. He could feel his heart beating inside his chest, and a rivulet of sweat had started to trickle its way down his spine.

"I hear that this connection of yours," said the Boss, "This *wealthy* connection, was quite an astute businessman. Would you agree?"

Another gulp.

"Erm… well, yes. Yes, he was, but –"

"But what?"

"He's dead, Boss. Passed away several years ago."

"You think I don't know that? Do you think I'm an idiot?"

"No, Boss, no, of course not. I was just saying, that's all."

"Word has it that when this *wealthy* connection shuffled off this mortal coil, he left everything to a certain half-brother of yours, while you got landed with – wait, don't tell me – ah, yes, now I remember: nothing. You got precisely nothing. Am I right?"

The man did not reply, but the sudden clenching of his jaw told the Boss that his assertion was correct.

"And so," he continued, "your dear brother now lives the life of Riley, with wealth unimaginable and everything his little heart desires, while you languish in this god-forsaken hole. Does this situation sit comfortably with you? I'm reliably informed that in all the time you've been stuck in here he hasn't been to visit you – not even once."

"No," came the muttered response. "He hasn't."

"Aww, ain't that a shame? Brotherly love can be such a wonderful thing."

"What do you want, Boss?"

"What do I want? What sort of question is that? I'm the one who's helping *you* here."

"How? How are you helping me?"

The Boss sighed.

"I thought I'd already explained that," he said. "I've

dropped a word in the appropriate ear, so you'll find the Parole Board will be very sympathetic to you. You'll be out of here in no time. Then, if you wanted, you could go and visit your brother. I'm sure he'd be delighted to see you. The two of you could have a wonderful time swapping news and catching up with all that's been happening."

"Very little has been happening for me in here."

"I know. That's the sad part, isn't it, but I'm sure someone of your intelligence could embellish the truth a little? Most guys in here do that all the time."

One of the guards in the tower had begun to look in their direction, but a pointed, icy glare from the Boss ensured that he quickly averted his gaze.

"It's very kind of you to help me like this, Boss, but once I'm out of this place my so-called brother will be the very last person I want to see."

Before the man quite realised what was happening, the Boss suddenly stepped forward again, and he found himself pinned between the barrel-like chest and the unyielding wall behind. The Boss grabbed the fabric of his prison-issue shirt in his two huge fists, causing the man to almost gag as a wave of bad breath emerged from between rows of yellow teeth and swept over him.

"What did you say your name was?" he hissed.

The man was almost choking.

"I didn't say," he spluttered. Then he cried out as the Boss swung his knee up firmly into his groin.

"I'll ask again. What did you say your name was?"

"Ma… Matthew," he said.

"Pardon? I didn't hear you – and call me sir."

"Matthew… sir. My name is Matthew."

"Hmm, that's better." The Boss released his grip on the terrified prisoner, smirking as he saw the patches of sweat which had begun to seep through his clothing.

"Maybe I wasn't clear," said the Boss, as he pushed Matthew roughly against the wall and took a step back, "And for that I apologise. So, for the avoidance of doubt, let me explain how this is going to go – and look at me when I'm talking to you; it makes me feel wanted."

Matthew lifted his head and looked into the cold, steely eyes of the colossus that stood before him.

"Do I have your attention?" he breathed.

"Yes, Boss... sir," came the subdued reply.

"Good. Now, listen. Although this wealthy individual of your acquaintance liked to give the impression that he had made his fortune through clever trading and shrewd business dealings, word has reached me that a not insubstantial portion of his income was derived from an altogether more unsavoury avenue. Do you understand me?"

"I'm sorry, sir. I'm not sure that I do."

"He liked to mix with high society. He knew all the film stars and always turned up at premieres and award ceremonies. He got to know those people well, *very* well. So much so that behind all the glitz and glamour he became aware of their – shall we say – more personal habits, the kind of things they wouldn't want the general public to know about. If certain things they'd been doing had come to light and found their way into the national papers their careers would have been ruined."

A split second before the Boss's next pronouncement, Matthew suddenly knew what he was about to hear.

"Your father," the Boss continued, "was a blackmailer."

"Surely not," he whispered.

"Wake up and smell the coffee, son," said the Boss. "Not only did your father have the rich and famous under his thumb, but this quaint little occupation of his operated on a large scale and was very effective. Of course, most of them are dead now, but their relatives were not best pleased when they learned about what had been happening, and why much of their expected inheritance had vanished. Well, it turns out they have 'acquaintances' of their own, and they now want to restore some order to the situation."

Matthew was struggling to take all this in, but the Boss continued.

"When you get out of here," he said, "you will go and find your brother, and you will 'persuade' him that he needs to share his spoils with you."

"Persuade him, Boss?"

"In due course, you will be contacted by an associate of mine who will provide you with details of the bank account into which you will deposit my share of the proceeds. I'm not an unreasonable man. Shall we say eighty percent?"

"Sir, how can I persuade him to part with all that money?"

"I will then apportion it, thereby ensuring that at least a little of his ill-gotten gains will be returned to the correct people, whilst also enabling me to take a small fee for all the trouble I have gone to in obtaining the guarantee for your release. Quite a reasonable price, in the circumstances – wouldn't you agree?"

"But he won't just hand over all that money, Boss."

Matthew gasped as a heavy fist planted itself deep in his solar plexus. Air whooshed from his body as he sank to the ground, his face a pale grey. The Boss stood over him, with a face like thunder.

"Listen," he hissed, "and listen well. I don't care whether he hands it over to you in gift wrapped parcels tied with pretty pink bows, or whether you have to gouge his eyes from their sockets to get it. Whatever method you choose is not my concern. Just make sure you have the money available when my associate contacts you, OK?"

Matthew looked down at the rough stone surface of the

quadrangle.

"I'll try," he whimpered, "But what if I can't manage it?"

"Oh, you'll manage it all right," said the Boss. "You'll manage it, cos if you don't you'll find yourself back in here in no time, where I'll be waiting for you – and you can safely assume that I won't be happy to see you. Do we understand each other?"

Matthew said nothing, but nodded.

"That's the spirit," said the Boss. Then he placed a large hand on the trembling man's shoulder. "Don't worry," he said, with a smile, "I'll be doing everything I can to help from inside here, and I have every confidence that you'll figure something out. Just don't let me down."

With that, he squeezed Matthew's shoulder, a little too firmly, then turned and walked away, with a casual swagger, back across the quadrangle and through a doorway where he disappeared inside the unwelcoming building.

Matthew sank down onto his haunches and leant back against the wall, breathing deeply, taking in great gulps of air. It was only now that he became fully aware of how much he was shaking. Glancing upward, and now that the Boss had gone, he saw that the guards in the tower had resumed watching him once again, with blank and impassive expressions.

CHAPTER 3

For several days, Charles continued to apply himself to his work as normal, though the cryptic message he had received was never far from his mind. Who on earth could have sent it? And to what end? Charles had racked his brain, but no one he could think of would have ever sent a note like that. Anyway, for the time being at least, there had been no further contact from the mysterious writer, so perhaps it was nothing more than a mischievous prank. It was probably some challenge or dare, dreamed up by a group of local tearaways who ought to be finding more constructive ways of spending their time. Yes, thought Charles, that was the most likely explanation.

The task of sorting through all of Lord Alfred's personal papers and other effects had turned out to be an enormous task. Years had passed, yet it was still ongoing.

Throughout the time Charles had been working as a solicitor, there had been numerous occasions when he had been asked by his clients how much time they should allow to completely settle the estate of a deceased loved one. In response, he would always refer to something called the 'executor's year'. Typically, this was the approximate period which would be needed to make certain that all details had been properly attended to, and that any loose ends had been finally tied up.

But that was for 'ordinary' people, who lived in an 'ordinary' house, who had owned 'ordinary' possessions and had an 'ordinary' bank account.

The estate of Lord Alfred Willoughby, however, had proved to be infinitely more complicated than that.

A little of the work had commenced soon after the occasion when the devious Lord had so convincingly faked his own death. As his dutiful solicitor, Charles had begun the task of sorting through the many official documents which he had been able to discover. However, this had naturally all come to an immediate halt once it emerged that Lord Alfred was still very much alive after all. Later, once nature had taken its course and the old fellow had finally departed – for real this time – the painstaking process of going through all those papers had begun again, and it quickly became apparent that this was a job which was going to take much longer than the standard 'executor's year'. True, much of the work had, by now, already been done, but Heston Grange was immense; there was a seemingly infinite number of rooms, and in some dark corner, there was always yet another filing cabinet or bureau waiting to be discovered which, inevitably, would be found to be stuffed with all manner of papers, documents, invoices, bills and receipts. Many of them were of no use at all and could be safely disposed of. Nevertheless, before throwing anything away, Charles had to carefully examine and scrutinise each individual item, just in case it should turn out to be something important. Consequently, the task felt as though it were taking an eternity to complete.

In particular, the contents of His Lordship's office – his

so-called 'secret' room in the octagonal tower – contained papers which were clearly significant, and there were a great many of them. The tower stood slightly separated from the main house, and it incorporated a most unusual design feature, the room, which was at second floor level, could only be accessed by means of a rickety bridge which linked the two structures, and it continued to be a constant source of irritation to Charles that he had to use it so many times. It was fashioned of ropes and thin strips of wood, and if there was the slightest breeze the bridge would sway and creak in a most unsettling way, and the wooden slats, which looked as though they would snap at any moment, would often become slippery in wet or frosty weather.

He was in the octagonal room now. Unlike the rest of the house, the tower had no electricity, and the room had no windows. This was a pity, since the bad weather which had lingered for several days had now abated. Although it was still chilly, Charles would have much preferred to be outside in the clear air, rather than shut up in this confined space. At the very least, a window to let in some natural light would have been most welcome. As it was, a single oil lamp stood on the desk, providing the only source of illumination and casting a semi-dull glow over the room and its contents. How Lord Alfred had been able to work in such gloomy conditions was a mystery to Charles

He was seated at what had been Lord Alfred's ornate writing desk, positioned in the middle of the floor and surrounded by filing cabinets and safes on almost every side. From one of these cabinets he had extracted a particularly weighty folder which now sat in front of him. As it turned out, it contained a wealth of correspondence and other documentation relating to his estate in Galloway where he had rented out a substantial number of properties. As far as Charles could tell, Lord Alfred's demise had in no way affected the regularity of the rental payments, which appeared to have continued regularly and reliably. He began to turn the pages, carefully scrutinising every detail. He did make progress, but it was dull work.

Periodically, he would pause and glance up at the only one of the eight walls which did not have a filing cabinet or safe pushed against it. Instead, here there was a small table, adorned with old, slightly grainy black and white photographs. These showed Lord Alfred with many famous celebrities and film stars of yesteryear, and there was even a picture of him attending one of the Oscar ceremonies.

Above the table, an old ceremonial sword hung on the wall, next to an antique clock, which ticked away remorselessly with perfect timing. Ah, he thought, as he looked at its hands with some feeling of relief, time for afternoon tea. That would be most welcome. In the past, James would have brought the tea to him (and, in all probability, some delicious homemade cake too) in the octagonal room, but Charles knew that negotiating the rickety bridge now posed too much of a challenge for the elderly servant. Instead, he had given the butler instructions to serve the tea in the conservatory.

Sure enough, just at that moment in one of the corners of the room a small bell hanging from a cord put forth a pleasant tinkle, letting Charles know that the tea was ready.

"Good old, James," he said, smiling to himself. "As regular as clockwork."

He picked up the large folder, tucked it under one arm and left the room, making his way across the swaying bridge and back into the main house once again, heading for his appointment with that much needed cup of piping hot tea.

✳✳✳

Charles had fully intended to continue his examination of the heavy folder with its stack of documentation while he took his tea. Despite his best intentions, though, as he gazed into the cheerful flames which sparkled and danced in the hearth before him, with cup and saucer in hand, the pile of official papers lay to one side, untouched, while he savoured the taste and reviving fragrance of the hot liquid which glided down and soothed his dry throat.

At length, as he was leaning forward towards the pot on the low table, and just about to pour himself a second cup, out of the corner of his eye he glimpsed the file which still waited alongside him. He sighed. After putting his cup down he reached out to pick up the folder but, before he had quite done so, the door opened and James entered the room, carrying the familiar silver tray upon which sat a cream coloured envelope.

"I'm sorry to disturb you, sir, but this just arrived for you and I thought you would want to see it straight away. It appears to be identical to the previous one, and it was again delivered to the back door, just like last time."

"And you didn't see who delivered it?"

The butler shook his head.

With a slight look of concern, Charles reached out and took the envelope. There was no question that it had come from the same source as before. His name was typed on the front in just the same way, and the envelope itself was made of the same textured paper.

For a moment, he almost asked James to remain on hand while he opened it, but then he decided it might be better if the contents were known to him alone, at least for now. So he waited, turning the envelope over and over in his hands, until the faithful manservant had departed and the door was safely closed.

Then, with both the tea and the large folder of documents

at his side temporarily forgotten, he slowly peeled back the flap of the envelope and slid out the contents.

Once again, there was just a single sheet of paper, folded in half.

Once again, the message was typed. There was no handwriting to be seen.

We haven't forgotten.
We are watching you.

***

At quite some distance from the house, down by the main gate at the end of the long drive, stood Heston Lodge. In days gone by this residence would have been home to the gatekeeper, but that role had been dispensed with a long time ago. These days, the lone occupant of the tiny dwelling seldom had visitors, though the habits of a lifetime ensured that each day she lit a fire in the reception room, and always had a supply of homemade cakes on standby. If anyone did happen to drop by she couldn't bear the thought of not being ready to show some hospitality and be a good hostess.

Today was no different. From the characterful chimneypot of this quintessentially English cottage, a tendril of smoke twisted and twirled its way heavenward in the clear air of the crisp, though rather cool, autumnal day.

A short distance outside the main gates, just beyond the bounds of the Heston estate and on the country lane which bordered it, a lone figure could be seen approaching. The figure, who walked with a pronounced limp, was wearing a padded anorak with the hood up. A thick scarf all but obscured the face of the walker and, although gloves were being worn, the hands were pushed firmly into deep pockets, in an attempt to stave off the cold air.

When the gateway to the Heston estate was reached the

figure stopped and peered through the wrought iron bars for a few moments. It was unlikely that there would be anyone to witness this arrival, but it was always wise to be careful.

Satisfied there was no one around, the figure produced a key and inserted it into the heavy padlock. A moment later, the primitive device sprang open, and the figure cautiously pushed against the heavy gate, easing it open a fraction. In the prevailing quietness, the sudden screeching of the unoiled hinges was startling. It sounded loud enough to have been heard in the next county, and caused a flock of alarmed birds in some nearby trees to take flight. The figure paused, waiting to see whether the sudden racket had attracted any attention.

There was nothing. Once the birds had departed, all was again quiet and still.

The figure stepped through the gap in the gates and, not wanting to risk any further unnecessary noise, left them standing open and headed towards the lodge.

The tiny building had in front of it a white picket fence with a small gate, both of which had once been in good condition, but with the passage of time their paintwork had grown old and tired, and was now flaking. Some of it had peeled away altogether, and glimpses of rotting wood could be seen beneath. As the figure pushed the gate open, it became apparent that it no longer fitted its space properly; the wood had absorbed moisture and expanded, causing it to scrape against the surface of the crazy paving pathway and preventing it from swinging open fully.

The figure took the few, lurching steps along the short path which led to the front door, and knocked. The door was made mostly of wooden panelling, but one of the panels was of glass, allowing the occupant to see who was there before opening it. There was no sound from within, and all the curtains were drawn, but the smoke from the chimney and a glow of light emanating from around the edges of the drapes indicated that the dwelling was occupied.

The visitor was about to knock again when a small, wizened face suddenly appeared in the door's glass panel. At first, the expression was blank, but after a few moments there was a sudden dawning of recognition and the face smiled. There was the sound of a bolt being drawn back, and the door was opened.

"Hello, Meg," said the visitor.

"Oh, what a nice surprise! How lovely to see you again," she said. "Is James with you?"

"Erm… no, sorry. He isn't."

"That's a pity. Ah well, never mind. Do come in. Kettle's on."

Meg led the way down the short, narrow hallway and into a cosy living room, furnished with an over-stuffed sofa and armchairs, and a small coffee table in the centre.

"Do sit down," she said. "I'll just fetch the tea."

As Meg slowly made her way through a narrow opening into the miniscule kitchen, the visitor disrobed, eased themselves into a seat and, just as on previous visits, surveyed the surroundings. Around the walls, the numerous shelves were filled with any number of small ornaments and pieces of bric-a-brac. Some of these objects were quite nice to look at, in themselves, but they did not appear to have been thoughtfully arranged. Rather, they seemed to have been all but thrown into their places, in some random, haphazard fashion, creating a somewhat cluttered appearance.

A couple of minutes later, Meg returned carrying a tray upon which cups, saucers and teaspoons rattled and tinkled against each other as she moved. She set it down on the small table in the centre of the room and regarded her guest.

"Now then," she said, "you'll have to remind me. Do you take both milk and sugar?"

"Yes. Milk and two sugars please."

"Lovely. That's just the way I like it myself."

As Meg was pouring the tea, the visitor noticed that there was no sugar bowl on the tray, but decided not to mention it.

"There we are," said Meg, as she offered the cup to her guest. "Drink it while it's hot."

"Thank you."

The visitor lifted the cup from its saucer and took a sip. The tea was stone cold.

"Aren't you going to have some?" the visitor asked.

"Perhaps in a while. I'm fine at the moment."

"Oh."

Meg settled herself in a chair and there was a pause as she regarded her visitor.

"Don't tell me," she said, abruptly. "It's Catherine, isn't it?"

"Actually, it's Kristin."

Meg clapped her hands in an expression of delight.

"Kristin! Of course it is, of course!" she exclaimed. "It is really most kind of you to come and visit. I trust the key to the gate proved useful. How have you been? You don't look very well. Did you hurt yourself?"

"I'm very well, thanks," Kristin replied. "Actually, there was something I wanted to ask you. I was wondering whether you had managed to find that journal we were talking about the last time I was here."

Meg didn't seem to hear.

"Naturally, I am very pleased to see you," she said, "but do you happen to know when James is going to visit? He said he would."

"I'm afraid I haven't seen James."

"Oh. I do miss him."

A silence.

"Meg, do you remember we spoke about a journal?"

"Did we? A journal? Did we, really?"

"Yes, the last time I came to visit you."

"A journal? Do you mean a magazine? I do always enjoy reading *Woman's Weekly*."

"No, Meg. This was a journal which had once belonged to Lord Alfred – a sort of diary."

"Oh, Lord Alfred! Now there was a fine man. A fine, upstanding man, and a true gentleman."

"The last time I was here I had hoped to meet with Charles Seymour, but you told me he was away – do you remember?"

Meg sat back in her chair. Her brow furrowed as she tried to recall their previous meeting.

"Instead, we talked about all sorts of things and had a very interesting chat. You told me about all the secret passageways in the house, and you also took me down into your cellar and showed me the entrance to the catacombs. Do you recall any of that?"

"Ah… maybe I do remember, though only vaguely – I'm not as young as I used to be, you know."

"And afterwards you told me you had heard of another hidden passage – one which only Lord Alfred knew about. You said that he spoke of it from time to time, but would steadfastly refuse to divulge where it was or how to get access to it."

A look of remembrance appeared on Megs face.

"Oh, yes," she said. "Yes, I think it's starting to come back to me now. Can you jog my memory with anything further?"

Her forehead wrinkled with the effort of trying to bring things to mind.

"Yes. You said he had told you that he had a back-up plan in case anything went wrong. He said it was a sort of insurance policy."

"I do remember now!" Meg proclaimed, as lucidity returned to her. "Yes, Lord Alfred said that he had managed to build up a kind of storehouse containing something that could be used in an emergency."

"That's right," said Kristin, "and you said you thought that it was probably a large quantity of money, or perhaps gold, kept in reserve in case times should ever become hard."

"Well, yes, but that was only a guess. As I mentioned, Lord Alfred never divulged even the location of this secret place – much less the contents – but I do know that he owned at least one gold mine, so it would seem to make sense, wouldn't it? He could safely squirrel away a good quantity of gold for possible future use, if needed, knowing that it could sit there for years without losing its value."

"That's quite correct," said Kristin.

"In fact," Meg continued, "I now recall Mr Seymour once telling me that he had used quite a slice of his inheritance to purchase a large number of shares in a diamond mine too – in South Africa, I think he said."

"Did he indeed? That is most interesting."

This was new information for Kristin which might prove useful later. For now, though, she was anxious to return to the main topic of conversation.

"Meg, do you remember when I spoke with you before, you told me that in case anything should happen to him, Lord Alfred had drawn up instructions for how to find this secret storehouse and written them down in his journal."

"Did I?" Meg's expression had gone a little blank again. "Oh, look, you haven't had your tea. Did I offer you a biscuit? Where's James?"

"I can ask him to come and visit you," said Kristin.

"Oh, would you? That is very kind."

"But before I do, could you tell me where Lord Alfred's journal is? It would really be most helpful if you can remember."

"Why do you need to know about it, anyway?" Meg's voice had suddenly taken on a sharp edge. What does Lord Alfred's secret have to do with you?"

"I'm a friend of Charles Seymour, and he asked me to try and find out whatever I could about it."

Meg considered this.

"Hmm. Well, I suppose that's all right then. It is nice of you to help Charles – he is such a kind man. He told me he would ask James to visit too, but he hasn't been to see me for such a long time."

Kristin cleared her throat.

"Meg, the last time I was here you said it was possible that you might have somehow brought Lord Alfred's journal with you when you moved here. You said it might be among all your things in one of those packing cases, down in the cellar."

Meg's eyebrows rose.

"I said that? Did I? I can't remember. Oh, but we can't go rummaging around down there. It's all dark and damp and there are dozens of boxes. It would take forever to search through them all."

Kristin did her best to remain calm.

"You said that you were going to try and find it for me."

"I did? Oh, I'm sorry. It must've slipped my mind. When you reach my age it's easy to forget things. Would you like some more coffee?"

"No, thanks. Listen, I don't want to be a burden to you. If it helped, and if you didn't mind, I would be happy to search for Lord Alfred's journal myself."

"What? Do you mean you want to go through all my belongings?"

"I assure you I would be very careful. Nothing would be damaged and I would replace everything exactly as I found it."

"Oh, but I wouldn't be comfortable with that. Those are my personal things. They are all very dear to me."

As Meg spoke, Kristen's jaw tightened, but she managed to remain calm.

"The thing is," she began, doing her best to maintain a measured tone, "Mr Seymour would very much like to see the journal as soon as possible. Do you think that if I came back to see you in a few days, you might have been able to find it for me by then?"

She smiled at the old lady in front of her, with a sweetness which she did not feel.

Suddenly, Meg's face brightened.

"Here's an idea!" she said. "On your next visit, why don't you bring James with you? *He* could help with the search. He's such a kind-hearted soul; I know he'd be willing to help, and also, –"

She paused, eyeing her visitor keenly, before continuing. "Please don't take offence, but… well, I don't actually know you that well. I would be much happier with *him* doing the searching."

"Yes, of course," Kristen replied, as she stood up. "I quite understand. I'll see what I can arrange. Thank you for your time. Don't worry – I'll see myself out."

"I'll have the kettle on waiting for you," Meg called after her.

There was the sound of the front door closing, followed by the departing uneven footsteps on the pathway outside, and Meg was alone again. She gazed into the middle distance, smiling and happy.

"James is coming!" she squeaked with excitement to the empty room. "Oh, how wonderful it will be to see him again."

CHAPTER 4

It was a bright morning and Charles was on his way down to the breakfast room. The long corridor had large windows down one side and, somehow, the sunlight streaming in brought a feeling of positivity and hope. Despite the fact that he had a long and probably dull day of scrutinising documents ahead of him, Charles found that he was walking briskly and with a spring in his step.

On impulse, and with a smile, he decided to take a different route to the one he normally took. At a certain point along the corridor he stopped and ran his fingertips around the edge of one of the wooden panels which lined the wall opposite the windows. After a moment, his fingers found the indentation he was searching for, with its concealed button within. He pushed it and, with a sharp click, the whole panel slowly swung back to reveal a darkened passageway behind. He reached out and flicked a switch. A row of bare light bulbs flickered into life and cast a harsh glare along the corridor.

Charles smiled again. This hidden thoroughfare ran behind the library. Many years ago, it was the very one from which Lord Alfred had secretly overheard Charles speaking with James after he had viewed the film containing details of the puzzle which would lead to the settling of his estate. How much had happened since then!

Of course, this was just one of the many hidden passages with which Heston Grange was riddled. This extraordinary residence had been quite deliberately designed with an irregular shape to facilitate the inclusion of these concealed corridors discreetly. However, despite undertaking some exhaustive research, Charles had been unable to discover who the original architect had been, or whether the house had been built with the specific intention of being a base for smuggling operations. All that *was* known was that the whole history of this sprawling mansion was shrouded in mystery, and Charles was only too aware that, in all probability, it contained still further secrets waiting to be discovered.

He walked the length of the concealed passageway swiftly, emerging through a similarly disguised doorway at the other end. As he stepped out into the main corridor he only narrowly avoided colliding with James, who was walking towards the breakfast room carrying a tray, whose contents were covered with a silver dome. The elderly butler was startled. He momentarily lost his balance, but managed to recover himself and prevent the contents of the tray from sliding off and onto the floor.

"James, I am so sorry," said Charles. "Are you all right?"

"Nothing to worry about, sir. No harm done. At least I managed to keep your breakfast on its plate. Mrs Gillcarey would never forgive me if I dropped it."

Mrs Gillcarey was a cook of superlative skill. Had she so chosen she could easily have become a very successful chef, but she had preferred, instead, to work as a housekeeper, firstly for Lord Alfred, and now for Charles. Now, she was long past retirement age, as was James, but over the years

Heston Grange had become so much a part of her that the thought of stopping work and leaving was one she could barely contemplate.

"When my time comes," she would say, every so often, "I want to go with my pinnie on."

That Mrs Gillcarey's gastronomic creations were sublime was beyond dispute. Consequently, whilst Charles would keep reminding her that she was welcome to stop work whenever she felt it to be appropriate, he was quietly hoping that the day would be as far into the future as possible. Privately, he even found himself wondering how he managed to remain so thin whilst consuming such a vast array of mouth-watering delights.

Charles followed James into the breakfast room and took his seat, while James transferred the domed plate to the table. This was one of Charles' favourite rooms. He loved it, especially on days like today, when the louvre windows were opened and the sunlight came flooding in. Once Charles had settled himself in the chair, James, with a flourish born of practiced fluency, lifted and swung the dome into the air to reveal the meal beneath.

And the meal did not disappoint.

This morning, the offering was smoked herrings with a fresh garden salad, and it looked superb. As James proceeded to pour him a cup of coffee, Charles eyed the feast before him, eagerly.

"Since we are favoured with such a bright morning, sir," said James, "Mrs Gillcarey thought that rather than a cooked breakfast, you might prefer a cold platter today."

Charles smiled. "James, as you well know," he began, "I am always delighted to devour anything which Mrs Gillcarey rustles up for me. She is a culinary genius!"

"I will be sure to pass on your compliment, sir. Please enjoy."

James set down the coffee pot and departed, while Charles set about his breakfast.

As a child, he had always felt salad to be a rather drab choice of meal, but that was before he had encountered Mrs Gillcarey. Somehow, she had the knack of turning a few simple leaves into a culinary masterpiece. Today, she had expertly blended some diced onions, with just the right quantities of Dijon mustard, lemon juice and olive oil to form a delicious dressing which coated the crisp lettuce, together with peeled, sliced tomatoes and cucumber. On the side were some haricot beans, seasoned with a hint of garlic, complementing the herrings beautifully, and the whole ensemble was sprinkled with freshly chopped basil and chives, straight from the garden.

It wasn't long before the plate was empty. Satisfied, Charles sat back in his chair and picked up the steaming coffee, savouring its comforting aroma before taking his first sip and gazing out through the open windows where, not far away, the waves of the ocean could be heard breaking, just beyond the cliffs.

***

Meanwhile, down in the kitchen below stairs, James had just finished telling Mrs Gillcarey about the warm welcome which her grilled herrings had been given. The two of them were now sitting at the large wooden table in the centre of the floor, and taking a short coffee break before returning to their daily duties.

They were both slightly startled when a knock was heard on the back door, at the end of the short passageway. Mrs Gillcarey glanced up at the clock.

"The butcher's early," she exclaimed. "I wasn't expecting him until noon, and I haven't even finished my coffee."

"Don't worry," said James, "I'll go."

Leaving his half empty mug, James rose to answer the knocking, as Mrs Gillcarey called after him. "Ask him to take all the meat straight to the pantry and just leave it on the side by the fridges. I'll come along in a minute to sort it all out."

As Mrs Gillcarey remained seated at the table, she listened to James' slow footsteps as he disappeared into the stone flagged corridor, and then heard the sound of the back door opening. Although she tried to hear, she was unable to make out the words of the ensuing conversation which, it seemed, was being spoken in hushed tones. This was unusual, since the butcher was a very jovial fellow with one of those loud, resonant voices which could always be heard clearly at quite some distance away.

With a curious and puzzled expression she was about to stand up to go and see what was happening, when the talking suddenly stopped. She heard the door close and then the unmistakeable sound of shuffling as James made his way back to the kitchen. When he emerged from the corridor he appeared to be deep in thought, and somewhat disconcerted.

"Why, Mr James," said Mrs Gillcarey, "I do declare you look as though you've seen a ghost! Is everything all right? What did the butcher have to say?"

James did not reply immediately. For a moment he placed his hands on the table and leaned against it, heavily, before then sinking down into the chair and taking a large gulp of his coffee.

"You poor thing," said Mrs Gillcarey, genuinely concerned. "Whatever is the matter? Are you unwell?"

James sighed and shook his head.

"That wasn't the butcher," he said.

"Well, I'd guessed that much. So… who was it?"

Speaking more quietly than usual, James answered, "It

was master Matthew."

Both of Mrs Gillcarey's hands came up to her mouth.

"Master Matthew?" she said, her voice little more than a whisper. "Oh, my… oh, my…." There was a long pause. Eventually, she spoke again. "Whatever did he say?" she asked.

"Not much. Only that he wanted to speak to Mr Seymour. He said that he felt nervous about approaching him directly and asked if there was some way I might be able to help to arrange a meeting between them."

"I had no idea he was out of jail."

"Neither did I. Even though he was always something of a scoundrel I did write to him while he was in there, but he didn't reply to any of my letters."

James pulled out a handkerchief and dabbed at his eyes, as Mrs Gillcarey, who was the salt of the earth, reached across the table and gave him an affectionate pat on the arm.

"Now then, don't you go upsetting yourself, you dear old thing," she said. "I'm sure he wanted to write back, but they have all sorts of rules and regulations about that sort of thing in prison, don't they?

James managed a weak nod.

"Perhaps," he said.

"Anyway," Mrs Gillcarey continued, "now he's out there won't be any need for letters, will there? You'll be able to speak to him whenever you like."

She gave a comforting smile, and James raised his head.

"Dear Mrs Gillcarey," he said, "whatever would I do without you?"

"Well, for a start, you'd have to make your own coffee," she said, with an endearing chuckle. "Would you like a top-up?"

James smiled.

"No, thank you. I think I should go and inform Mr

Seymour that his… ahem… half-brother would like to see him."

"Oh, my," said Mrs Gillcarey. "I wonder what he wants to talk about? I do hope there's not going to be any problem. Mr Seymour is such a fine gentleman. I couldn't bear the thought of him having any trouble."

"He didn't say why he wanted to see him, and I didn't feel comfortable asking. He did appear to be suitably contrite, but with Matthew you never quite know what's going on inside that mind of his." There was a silence as James lapsed into thought for a moment, but then he stirred himself. Standing up from the table, he spoke again. "Ah well, I did tell him I would alert Mr Seymour to his request, so I suppose I had better go and do it."

***

Following his satisfying breakfast, Charles had now safely traversed the rickety bridge and was back inside the room in the octagonal tower. The huge stacks of files and folders which awaited him, all of which were stuffed with a myriad of documents of many kinds, were, to say the least, very daunting.

One of these piles had been extracted from a formidable-looking safe which stood against the wall directly in front of the desk, and whose door, with the bunch of keys still dangling from the lock, stood open, revealing a dark interior lined with black velvet. As Charles was reaching towards the first stack of folders to commence his work, something about the open safe caught his eye. He couldn't quite place what it was, yet something had registered in his subconscious and was trying to fight its way through into his conscious mind. He paused and looked at the safe more carefully. By the dim light of the oil lamp it was not easy to see into its every recess from where he sat, yet he had come to recognise and trust moments like these, where his instinct was trying to tell him something.

With his arm still outstretched towards the pile of documents he looked over at the safe again. He still saw nothing out of the ordinary, yet his curiosity had somehow been awakened. Thoughts of all those files and folders were temporarily pushed aside, as he stood up and walked round to the other side of the desk. Carefully, he picked up the oil lamp and, holding it aloft, he crouched in front of the open safe and peered inside.

The several shelves within this large receptacle were still occupied with various items and numerous sheets of yet-to-be-examined paper, but there was nothing especially untoward here.

So what was it that had arrested his attention?

Ah, it was probably nothing. Maybe he had just been working too hard.

Charles sighed and was about to turn away, when he suddenly saw what his subliminal mind had already picked up on.

There, almost out of sight, and set into the floor of the safe towards the back, was a small silver ring. With a feeling of excitement, all thoughts of the waiting piles of dusty documents were forgotten as Charles reached into the safe, slipped his finger inside the ring, and gently pulled. Slowly, a portion of the floor of the safe began to lift, revealing a hidden compartment beneath. Charles gasped as he began to glimpse something lying in the dark cavity.

Don't get too excited, he told himself. It's probably yet another boring old invoice file, or some such thing. Yet still he found himself trembling a little, as he reached into this newly discovered space to retrieve what lay within.

As his fingers made contact with the item Charles was

slightly surprised to find that it felt slightly soft to the touch. Taking hold of the object, he carefully lifted it out and examined it.

It appeared to be some sort of notebook. It was approximately eight inches high by six wide, and it had a textured, beige moleskin cover. Carrying the book reverently, Charles returned to the desk and set it down, before easing himself into his chair. For a long moment he regarded the closed book in front of him, savouring the moment. What did the book contain? What was he about to discover?

Slowly, he reached out and opened it.

He found that the first page was covered in handwriting. It was very elaborate and distinctive, and Charles immediately recognised it as being that of Lord Alfred.

And it appeared to be some sort of poem.

Charles felt his pulse quicken, and in his mind he was immediately whisked back to the treasure hunt upon which he had embarked many years ago – a hunt in which a certain poem had played a very prominent role. Surely what now lay before him couldn't be yet another set of cryptic clues, could it?

By the less-than-ideal light from the oil lamp, the excited Charles at first skimmed through the poem quickly, but he did not really assimilate any of the detail; so then he read it again, more slowly and carefully this time, though even the title was a source of vexation for him:

The Falchion points the way

Behind the tree lies a sun-bleached stone
Near or far, 'tis still called home
Ah! Ne'er more earnest was it meant
Hither and thither the boy was sent

41

Hoping! Yes, kept hope alive
Or sustained an outcome tragic
Trying to pursue acacia
Growing old with super ego

Nearly missed the old enigma
Latent not, away it went
Opened, then, fair fortune's window
Entered, there, a greater power

Charles sat back in the chair and rubbed his eyes. What on earth did this mysterious piece of writing mean? Indeed, did it mean anything at all? Or was it simply a poem that Lord Alfred had liked so much that he had just copied it out, in much the same way as he had done with numerous others which Charles had previously discovered on the library shelves in years gone by?

Hmm.

And yet, if this piece of verse held no real significance why had Lord Alfred gone to the trouble of not just locking it away in a safe, but of also further concealing it inside an inner secret compartment?

His gaze fell once again on the opening of the last stanza: *Nearly missed the old enigma*. Charles sighed. Nearly missed it? Chance would be a fine thing! He knew he was nowhere near it and, if he was honest with himself, Charles just didn't have the energy to embark on yet another round of clue-solving.

With a feeling of weariness, he turned the page – and found another surprise waiting for him.

Here was yet more of Lord Alfred's spidery script, only this time it was not a poem. It was a letter. Charles took a deep breath, and began to read.

To whom it may concern:

Greetings.

Naturally, I do not know who will read this letter. However, since you have managed to locate this book and its contents I am hoping that I may consider you to be more of an ally than an enemy. Nevertheless, I cannot be absolutely certain, so I have endeavoured to take certain precautions.

The difficulty I am facing is this: Over the course of my life, the fact that I managed to amass such a considerable fortune inevitably caused certain problems to follow along in its wake. At this stage of life I am too old and tired to fight or hide anymore, so I have to hold up my hands and admit that some of my business dealings were — shall we say — a little less than ethical. I thought I had taken ample measures to cover my tracks, but for some time I have had reason to believe that certain undesirable persons are wishing to find me, in order to try and extract from me what they perceive to be their due. Now, if I am lucky, I think that I may yet safely depart this life before anything unpleasant occurs. However, it is for YOU, the reader of this letter, that I am concerned. Those who are now engaged in searching for me are most unscrupulous, and will not think twice about coming after you instead, if they feel it necessary in order to secure their interests.

I have therefore put something in place which, in the event that the worst should happen, will hopefully supply a resolution. I have to concede that my contingency plan is not ideal. However, in the circumstances I believe it to be the best I can do. At the very least, it certainly outshines certain other possible outcomes which would be too horrifying to contemplate.

Having said that, I need to ensure that my 'surprise' is discovered

43

only by the right person. Therefore, I have concealed its location within the poem on the previous page. Are you, the reader of this letter, for me or against me? I have no way of knowing, but I will say this: If you are the right person to solve this little conundrum you will know how to do it.

I wish you well.

Charles leaned back and released a long, deep breath. He read and re-read the letter several times, and then he turned the page back and looked at the poem again too.

What he had read had given him a deeply unsettling feeling. What did the letter and its accompanying poem mean? Charles didn't have the slightest idea. In that case, according to Lord Alfred's letter, it meant that he was not the right person to uncover the location of this mysterious surprise, whatever it was. So, in one sense, that let him off the hook. On the other hand, though, what about these 'undesirable persons' who were mentioned? What should he now be doing? Should he be trying to find the answer to this enigmatic riddle, or not? What would happen if these unscrupulous individuals came calling, and Charles knew what and where Lord Alfred's surprise was? On the other hand, what if they came calling and he *didn't* know?

He leant forward onto the desk, and put his head in his hands.

CHAPTER 5

With so many thoughts crowding into his mind Charles wasn't quite sure how long he'd been sitting there. In fact, he had almost slipped off into a doze, when he was suddenly jarred back to full wakefulness by the sound of the bell ringing in the corner. He glanced at the clock, and a puzzled look crossed his face. The bell was, generally, only used by James to let him know that the next meal or pot of tea was ready, but right now was not the usual time of day for either of those.

The beige notebook, containing both the unsettling letter and the problematic poem, still lay open on the desk in front of him. Closing it, he stood up and tucked it under his arm. He then left the room, making his way back over the rickety bridge and into the main house once again.

A few minutes later found him walking into the conservatory. A quick glance about the room revealed the unsurprising fact that there was no refreshment waiting for him, but his loyal butler was there, standing respectfully.

"A bit early for lunch, isn't it?" Charles asked.

"I do apologise for disturbing you, sir," said James. "I am

fully aware that the bell is not a tool with which to summon you. After all, it is you who arc the master of the house, while I am a mere menial."

"Come now, James, don't put yourself down. I know you wouldn't have used the bell unless it was for something important."

James nodded. "You are quite correct, sir." He fidgeted, uncomfortably.

"Well then," said Charles, "what is it?"

James cleared his throat.

"It would appear," he said, "that master Matthew has been released from prison."

Charles' mouth fell open.

"Has he, indeed? How long has it been now?"

"Almost ten years, sir."

"Time certainly flies. I'd virtually forgotten him."

"I hadn't, sir."

"No, of course not. I'm sorry, James."

"Sir… a short time ago, master Matthew was here."

"Here? At the house?"

James nodded.

"He came to the back door, sir, where we had a short conversation."

"Whatever did he want?"

"Actually, sir, he was asking me whether I thought you might be willing to see him."

In a flash, memories of all that had happened with Matthew almost a decade ago suddenly re-emerged. Charles had thought that these had all been dealt with, and filed away in some dark corner of his mind, nevermore to be thought of. Yet now, all of a sudden, here they were, back again, large as life and just as vivid as they were at the moment when they had actually occurred: the way Matthew had responded when he first learned of thc contest involving the cryptic lines; the decision he and Charles had reached to work together to solve the clues; his moment of betrayal at the end of the quest, and the final denouement down in the crypt; the subsequent court case and, finally, the extraordinary revelation that Matthew had not been Lord Alfred's son at all, but was, in fact, the child of James and Meg.

"Sir?"

"Hmm? Oh, I'm sorry, James, I was miles away – just remembering all those things from before, you know?"

"Quite so, sir. I don't wonder at it."

"So, Matthew wants to see me?"

"He does, indeed, sir."

"Do you know why?"

"He didn't say, and I didn't like to ask – I must confess that I felt a little overcome when he suddenly appeared like that, unannounced."

"Well, I'd be happier if I knew what he wanted, and I somehow don't think he wants to come just to have a nice little chat over a cup of tea."

"You never know, sir. I well recall what a scoundrel he has been in the past, but perhaps his time inside has given him opportunity for reflection. Maybe he wants to patch things up and make amends."

"Do you really believe that?"

James paused and looked at the floor, a little crestfallen.

"I don't know, sir," he said, with a sigh, "though I would very much like to."

"Well, if the leopard has indeed changed his spots, I suppose that can only be a good thing. All right, James, I'll see him, though I need to make some more progress with my work first. Could you find out from him when he is available? Perhaps we could invite him for morning coffee at the weekend?"

"Very good, sir. I'll arrange it."

No sooner had James left the conservatory than Charles realised he had forgotten to mention the beige notebook. He was about to call after him, but then changed his mind. Instead, he took a seat and began to read through both the letter and the poem again.

It was about fifteen minutes later when Charles heard in the distance the sound of the front doorbell ringing. Shortly after that, James re-entered the conservatory.

Charles was a little frustrated at having his concentration broken so soon, but he closed the book and looked up at his faithful butler.

"Well, sir, it seems that you are proving to be most popular today. I was about to call master Matthew as you instructed, but was interrupted by the arrival of another visitor. There is now a lady here to see you."

"A lady? Who is it?"

"She wouldn't give her name, sir. She would only say that she knows you from years ago and that she had something important to tell you, which was for your ears only!"

"Sounds a bit suspicious."

"Indeed, sir – almost like something straight out of an espionage film."

"Oh, very well. Where is she?"

"I've shown her into the drawing room, sir."

"All right. I'll be there in a minute."

"Very good, sir."

A moment after the door had closed, Charles realised that, yet again, he had neglected to mention the notebook to James. This was doubly irksome, since it had been lying open on his lap the whole time. He gave an audible gasp of exasperation. Setting the book to one side, he stood up and began to make his way to the drawing room to see this unexpected, mysterious visitor.

***

Once again, it was exercise time and the grey, featureless quadrangle was filled with inmates. As always, some were engaged in a variety of physical activities, either individually or in small groups, while others passed the time by making casual conversation, leaning against the walls or sitting on the steps by the doorway.

The one person not taking advantage of this opportunity for social interaction was the Boss. This hulk of a man walked slowly round the concrete area, following a roughly circular route, saying nothing but deep in thought. Somehow, he always found it easier to think out here, where he could walk, rather than while being cooped up in the confines of his cell.

Other inmates, on seeing him approaching, and knowing better than to get in his way, would nudge each other, and then quietly move aside so as not to disturb either his progress or his thought process.

Amongst his other current 'projects', the Boss found himself mostly wondering about how a certain Matthew Willoughby was getting on with the task which had been set for him. There had been no word, as yet.

The Boss felt his jaw tighten.

He didn't like to be kept waiting.

He had better hear something, and soon.

***

When Charles first entered the drawing room it appeared to be empty.

Puzzled, he was about to pull the cord to summon his butler when he noticed the woman, partly obscured by the thick, hanging drapes, standing in the bay window and looking out over the grounds. Charles cleared his throat.

"Hello," he said. "Can I help you?"

The figure did not reply, but continued to stand facing the window, creating an awkward silence which Charles found distinctly uncomfortable.

"Hello?" he said, again.

This time, there was a reply, though the speaker still did not turn round.

"It's been a long time, Charles."

The voice was certainly familiar, though Charles couldn't quite place it.

"Erm… I'm afraid you have me at a disadvantage," he said.

"I don't blame you for not recognising me," the woman said. "The last time we saw each other I looked a little… well, different."

"To be honest, it is fairly unlikely that I would recognise anyone from behind."

The figure gave a snort.

"Probably true," she said. "Very well, then."

And, with that, the figure turned round, though the process of doing so was not a smooth one. Rather, it appeared to be a somewhat cumbersome combination of limping and lurching.

The figure was now facing Charles, but it was still impossible to make out the identity, since the visitor's face was largely covered by a scarf.

"You're not making this easy," said Charles.

The woman sighed, and then began to unwind the long piece of brightly coloured fabric.

Charles gasped. The visitor was correct, on two points. Firstly, they had met before, a long time ago. Secondly, though she was recognisable, her appearance had markedly changed.

"Kristin," he said, his voice barely above a whisper.

"Well done," she said. "In that case, perhaps I don't look quite so different after all?"

But she did.

Kristin was hugely disfigured. At some point in the past, she had suffered two serious gash wounds to her face; the ugly, tell-tale scars ran diagonally, almost in parallel, from the top left of her forehead, across her nose and cheeks, and finally ending just below her chin. The skin surrounding her left eye was stretched tight, preventing it from opening fully, and giving her features a lop-sided appearance.

Charles did his best to disguise the feelings of revulsion which swept over him, and managed to maintain his composure.

"You won't be surprised to learn that I decided to withdraw from my local beauty contest," said Kristin, with a sarcastic sneer.

Charles could hardly speak, and wasn't sure what he should say anyway. Yet, somehow, after a long and awkward silence, a question managed to force its way out from between his lips.

"Kristin… what happened?"

"Ha. Why should you care what happened?"

"Why should *I* care? If I remember correctly, you were the one who stopped caring."

Many years ago, Charles and Kristin were planning to be married. At least, Charles had thought they were. The date had been set, the many necessary arrangements were well underway, and everything had seemed to be progressing wonderfully.

How quickly it had all changed.

One morning – Charles could recall it as clearly as if it had happened yesterday – Kristin had walked into the kitchen and calmly announced, in a way that was almost formal, that she was leaving. Then, without a word of explanation to her open-mouthed ex-fiancé, she picked up her already-packed bag of belongings and simply walked out.

For Charles, that moment became frozen in time. Even now, he could still see himself seated at the breakfast table, which he had set for two. The bright sunlight, which had been foretelling a very pleasant day, was quite at odds with the bad news he was now trying to assimilate. The rays streamed in through the window, glinting and reflecting in the gleaming cutlery. The slice of toast, which was halfway to his mouth when Kristin had delivered her announcement, slipped from his fingers and fell back onto the plate, uneaten.

There had been no forewarning, no indication that anything was amiss. On that fateful day she had simply departed, giving no reason, and Charles had been left devastated.

"Do you realise," he whispered, battling with a mixture of internal emotions, "that after you walked out I couldn't move. I sat there for more than two hours, staring across the table at your empty chair and the cup of coffee I had made for you?"

"I'm very sorry," she said, and it almost sounded as though she meant it. "I thought it would be easier for you if I did it quickly."

"I see. So I'm supposed to think that you were doing me a favour?"

"No. It wasn't like that."

"Then please enlighten me. I'm all ears."

There was a long pause. The air of expectancy which hung in the air was almost palpable.

"I made a mistake," she said, at last.

Another silence.

"I appreciate your candour. So… is that it? Is that what you wanted to say?"

"Don't mock me, Charles! This is hard enough for me as it is. May we sit down?"

"Please do."

He indicated the two armchairs on either side of the fireplace. Kristin limped towards one of them and eased herself into it. Charles sat opposite, and the two of them then gazed at each other. He felt an inner compulsion to tell her to hurry up and get on with whatever she had come to say, but decided it would probably be better if he were to let Kristin take her time. Eventually, she spoke again.

"I was always deeply fond of you," she said.

"That's nice. I thought it was more than that. I thought we were in love."

"So did I. I mean… yes. Yes, we were. At least…."

"Yes?"

"Oh, Charles, you were a solicitor."

"I still am. So what?"

"You were always so calm, so stable, so regular and dependable… and so… oh, so predictable."

"Ah, so I wasn't interesting enough for you?"

"When Gerald first appeared in my workplace, he swept me off my feet. He was young, good looking, chivalrous and… well… exciting."

"Congratulations. You were obviously made for each other."

Kristin ignored the sarcasm and continued.

"Hardly a day would go by without a meeting, or a phone call at the very least, and then there were all the bouquets and chocolates."

"And jewellery?"

"Oh, yes. Lots of lovely bracelets and necklaces, and –"

She stopped speaking, realising she had said too much.

"It all sounds perfect. So what went wrong?"

Kristin sighed.

"I'm not the first girl in history to be swayed by the trappings of wealth and charisma," she said, "and I know I won't be the last. I was wrong to allow myself to be enticed so easily – I know that now – but, by the time I discovered what sort of man Gerald really was on the inside, it was too late."

"Your face," said Charles, gently. "Did he do this to you?"

She did not reply, but gave a slight, almost imperceptible nod.

"I really tried to be the person he wanted me to be, but nothing was ever good enough for him, and when he became angry it was just –"

She paused for a moment, before resuming, more quietly, "– awful. It was awful. Each time, he would apologise afterwards and say he loved me, and promise he'd never do anything like that again. Then another bunch of flowers would arrive, even bigger than the last one, and I – fool that I was – would decide to give him another chance."

As Charles listened, he found, to his surprise, that he was feeling sorry for her.

"Would you like a drink?" he asked.

"No. Thank you." Kristin summoned her nerve, took a deep breath and continued. "One day he pushed me down the stairs. I fell badly and was in excruciating pain, but he wouldn't call an ambulance. He insisted on taking me to the hospital himself, telling me all the way that he 'loved me so much'. Once we arrived he left me at the entrance because he had to go to work – he had an important meeting, he said. They took some X-rays and found that both my ankles were broken in several places. The doctors did their best to patch me up, but warned me that it was unlikely I would be able to walk normally in future. Now, periodically I have to go back for a check-up. They tell me that I'm doing very well, since I can hobble along without a stick, so I suppose I should be grateful for that."

"What happened after you left the hospital?"

"In a way, the fall down the stairs was a wake-up call. Admittedly, it came late, but better late than never. I knew I had to get out of there. So, I did my planning, chose my moment and, one day, while he was out I packed what few things I could carry and left."

"Left? Just like that? The same as you did with me." Charles immediately regretted his words. "I'm sorry," he said, "I shouldn't have said that."

"It's all right," she said. "I suppose I deserved it."

"Well," Charles said, "you may not want a drink, but I certainly need one."

He crossed over to the cabinet on the far side of the room and poured himself a large whiskey.

Kristin allowed herself a slight smile.

"So in my absence you've graduated onto strong drink?"

"Not as a rule, no."

From where he stood, Charles regarded the unfortunate creature before him and felt a genuine surge of pity. Before, when they had been together and the future had seemed so bright, she had been so elegant, so divine and so perfect. Yet now….

"Kristin," he said, finally, "how did you know I lived here, and why have you come to see me?"

"The first answer is easy. *Everyone* knows you live here. All that business with Lord Alfred's Will and Matthew's trial was all over the news."

"Fair enough, and the second answer?"

There was a pause, as Kristin hesitated. She shuffled her deformed feet and looked at the floor.

"Charles," she said, at last, "I need to ask a favour of you, but please do not feel under any obligation. I know that the way I treated you was appalling, and I will quite understand if you do not feel able to assist me."

"Very well. I'll defer my decision until I hear what your request is."

"Spoken like a true solicitor."

CHAPTER 6

The next morning, the day was again bright and sunny, so Charles had decided to go for a walk. He needed some space to sort through all that was pressing in upon his mind, and to clarify his thinking.

Despite the sunlight, though, the exposed clifftops tended to be quite windy, so Charles was glad that he had remembered to don his thick coat. Carrying his shoulder bag, he strolled along the grass-topped ancient cliffs, gazing out over the endless sea and listening to the gulls screeching, as they hovered overhead before suddenly swooping down to snatch a tasty morsel from the waters below.

Until very recently, Charles thought to himself, other than the ongoing erosion of the chalk cliffs by the relentless ocean, everything had seemed to be sailing along on a more or less even keel.

Now, however, in the space of a few short days, he found himself engulfed by waves of complexity. Firstly, there had been the discovery of Lord Alfred's journal, containing the letter and the cryptic poem. Charles wasn't sure he had the stomach for another blasted treasure hunt, yet the letter had a sinister undertone which suggested that it really would be in his interest if he could locate the cleverly hidden surprise to which both the letter and mysterious poem alluded.

Then there was the arrival of those anonymous and sinister notes. Were they linked to Lord Alfred's poem in some way? Since they were delivered by hand and not by regular mail, this indicated that some stranger was wandering around in the grounds at will. That was disconcerting enough, but now there was even more to occupy his thoughts: right out of the blue, Matthew had been released early from prison and wanted to speak to him. Why?

And then, to cap it all, just when he had almost managed to assimilate all these things, his ex-fiancé re-appeared, maimed and disfigured, like some hideous ghost from the past, re-awakening memories and plunging him back into the emotional turmoil from which he thought he had recovered.

Out here, the scenery was beautiful. Charles always liked walking here. Yet, today he didn't really see anything. The demands on his mental faculties were such that he didn't know what to think about first. All of a sudden, there was just too much going on. It had all become too complicated, and some simplification was needed.

But how to go about it?

In essence, what Kristin had come to ask him was whether she could stay at Heston Grange – just temporarily, until she could arrange accommodations which would be more suitable for someone in her condition and circumstances. She also needed somewhere which was suitably close to amenities – which Heston Grange certainly wasn't. At first, Charles feared that she might have been hoping to move in permanently, but she had made it quite clear that this was not the case; for a start, it was not easy for her to manage staircases. In addition, whilst there had been no problem with finding a room for her on the ground floor, her difficulties with walking meant that the house was just too large to be practical.

Charles had even found himself wondering whether Kristin had returned in the hope of re-kindling the old romantic flame between them. This thought had now occurred to him several times but, as he stood on the rocky promontory, staring out over the wild ocean beneath, he knew there was no chance of that happening. She had given no indication that she still had feelings for him and, if he was honest, he realised that he too had moved on.

Alone with the sky and the waves, he gave a rueful smile. Before, it would probably have worked, he said to himself, but that was then.

Years ago.

Things were different now.

Whenever he walked along the high cliffs there was a particular place where he would always pause. He reached that place now, and sat himself down on a large, white, flat rock set into the otherwise grassy surface. Usually, he would stare into the horizon, and drink in the natural beauty, basking in the openness and vast expanse of the billowing clouds. Today, though, reaching into his bag, he pulled out Lord Alfred's journal and, turning his back to the wind to avoid the risk of damage to the pages, he opened it, and re-read the poem and letter for the umpteenth time.

He was dismayed to find that he was still none the wiser.

A sun bleached stone. This was the second time that such a stone had been mentioned, since it had also appeared in the original poem years ago. Was there some connection there? And, as mentioned in the letter, what was the identity of these 'undesirable persons' who might decide to pay him a visit? Charles had no idea.

At length, and with a sigh, he returned the book to his bag, stood up and began to head back towards the house, walking away from the churning waters below.

***

When the weekend arrived, Charles awoke early, feeling both nervous and excited.

The last time he had seen Matthew Willoughby was as he watched him being sent down to the cells after what had been a very difficult and emotionally draining trial; now, all these years later, the man suddenly wanted to make contact again.

Inwardly, Charles had very mixed feelings about this. In the past, he had trusted him; he had taken him into his confidence; they had struck a deal and agreed to work together.

And then, at the last moment, Matthew had betrayed him.

It was only the timely intervention of Lord Alfred which had prevented an altogether more unpleasant outcome. Surely the sensible thing would have been simply to decline his request to meet?

Well, yes, of course it would.

And yet… and yet….

From hearing James' account of his conversation with Matthew a few days ago, it did seem like a distinct possibility that the man really had changed and now wanted to 'clear the air', to lay the past to rest and make a fresh start. If that was the case, didn't he deserve to be given a second chance? Surely everyone deserved that, didn't they?

But was it really possible?

Despite all Matthew's faults and involvement with shady characters in the past, could it be that he had truly reformed? Both Charles and James wanted to believe it but, after all their previous experience, they knew that it would be wise to proceed with caution.

Ah, well, thought Charles to himself, let's not jump to any hasty conclusions until we've heard what Matthew has to say for himself.

The appointment had been arranged for 10am. It was yet another bright morning, and unusually warm for the time of year, so Charles decided that it might be helpful if the meeting took place outside on his favourite patio. Hopefully, the tranquil setting would create a relaxed mood, and be more appropriate to the needs of the moment than the more formal setting of his study or one of the other rooms.

So the plan was made. Once Matthew had arrived, James would bring him along to the patio, where Charles would be laying on a recliner and reading a newspaper. Shortly afterwards, James would return bringing some coffee. Everything would be done to try and make the visit as easy and as smooth running as possible for everyone. Who knows, thought Charles, if we're really lucky perhaps there might even be some birdsong to add to the overall ambience.

Deep down, though, Charles wasn't at all sure whether his efforts to create a relaxed environment were primarily for Matthew's benefit or for his own. At the appointed time, when he heard the sound of a car arriving he felt his heartbeat speed up, and he did his best to try and hold the newspaper still, without the pages showing any obvious signs of shaking.

A couple of minutes later, he heard the sound of approaching footsteps, and James announced, "Matthew Willoughby to see you, sir."

James stood to one side, allowing Matthew to step out through the open doors and onto the patio. He was now slightly thinner than Charles remembered – a little more gaunt, perhaps? – and his face had just started to display a few wrinkles. Nevertheless, he was clearly recognisable and, with a wash of memories suddenly flashing through his mind, Charles felt an involuntary shudder as he stood up to welcome him.

Affecting a smile, he walked towards Matthew, with his hand extended. He had hoped that the first moment of their meeting would be convivial and friendly. However, in reality it felt rather stilted and awkward, and the handshake was very brief indeed.

"Hello, Matthew," he said, trying to sound pleased to see him.

"Hello, Charles," came the equally unconvincing reply.

"Would you like to sit down?"

"Yeah, thanks."

At first, no further words were spoken at all. Desperate to say something – *any*thing – Charles had been on the point of asking Matthew how prison life had treated him, but then at the last moment decided that that was a question which was better left unasked, at least for now. So, the two of them simply sat there, avoiding eye contact and looking around at the many varieties of plants and flowers which surrounded them. Fortunately, on the branch of a tree somewhere nearby, an obliging trio of sparrows had begun to chirp, helping to dispel what would otherwise have been a very uncomfortable silence. Even when James arrived with the coffee, it was served with no sound other than the tinkling of cups, saucers and teaspoons.

Eventually, it was Charles who tried to break the ice.

"It was good of you to come, Matthew," he said. "I'm glad to see you."

Matthew looked up.

"Are you, Charles? Are you really? It's nice of you to say

so, but I know I didn't exactly cover myself in glory the last time I was here."

Charles didn't reply, directly. Instead, he gave what he hoped was a sympathetic smile. Reaching forward, he picked up one of the cups of coffee and held it out to him. As Matthew took it, Charles spoke again, gently. "What can I do for you, Matthew? What prompted you to contact me again?"

Matthew took a deep breath before replying.

"First and foremost," he began, "now that I'm out of jail I want to put the past behind me and make a fresh start. I've learned my lesson and I have no wish to end up back in there again."

"I'm very glad to hear that," said Charles. "As one of my old schoolteachers used to say, the only lesson wasted is the one you learn nothing from."

Matthew gave half a smile. He was clearly not finding this conversation to be an easy one, but he persevered and continued. "Also," he said, "I wanted to see you to personally apologise for all the hurt and distress I caused before."

Inside, Charles didn't really know the best way to respond to this. The 'hurt and distress' to which Matthew referred, was something of an understatement, to put it mildly. If he was honest, something deep inside Charles wanted to walk over to Matthew and punch him firmly in the face.

However, the events of the past had all taken place many years ago, and Matthew did seem to be genuinely penitent, so Charles was only a little surprised when he heard himself say, "We all take a different path through life, and along the way we find that we have decisions to make. Sometimes we make the right choices, and sometimes we make mistakes. I very much appreciate what you have said, and I am happy to let bygones be bygones."

Matthew exhaled, deeply, and appeared relieved.

"Thank you," he said.

There was another pause. As they both sipped their coffee, the sunlight glinted through the boughs of the trees, and sound of the birds singing somehow seemed sweeter now. A minute later, James re-appeared, carrying a fruit cake, which looked very appealing, and two plates.

"Mrs Gillcarey sends apologies for the slight delay with this," he said. "It hadn't quite finished baking, but here it is now, fresh and still hot from the oven. She hopes you will enjoy it."

"It looks wonderful," said Charles. "Please give our thanks to Mrs Gillcarey."

"Very good, sir. I will."

As James began to slice and serve the cake, Charles spoke again.

"So, now that you are a free man once again, do you have any immediate plans?"

"Sort of. I mean, yes. Yes, I do. I'm hoping to try and find a job. That is, if anyone will take me."

"That's very good news," said Charles. "I know that would make your father extremely happy."

As he spoke, he glanced at James and detected the most momentary of pauses in his slicing of the cake, and was that just a tiny hint of a proud smile? However, the extent, if any, to which his professional persona may have slipped was swiftly recovered. A few moments later, having placed a slice of the homemade delicacy in front of each of them, James departed once more, walking, Charles thought, with a fraction more spring in his step than was usually the case these days.

After a few moments, Matthew put down his plate and cleared his throat.

"Actually," he said, adopting a serious tone, "I'm afraid

there is something else I need to tell you."

As he heard those words, Charles felt an involuntary sinking feeling in the pit of his stomach. Endeavouring to maintain a calm outward demeanour, he pushed his plate and cup to one side and tried to smile.

"I'm all ears," he said.

So Matthew began.

He told him all about the way his early release from prison had come to pass. He told about the Boss, an extremely unpleasant character full of threats and intimidation, and about how this hulk of a man had, apparently, spoken to the parole board on his behalf.

And then he explained what the Boss was expecting in return, not forgetting to mention that an 'associate' of the Boss would be contacting him soon to find out what progress had been made.

As Charles gradually began to realise the extent of the situation which now faced him, his entrails felt as though they were turning to water. He hadn't felt like this since the critical events which had taken place down in the crypt all those years ago. Like a thunderbolt, the anonymous messages in their cream coloured envelopes returned to his mind in sharp focus. Suddenly, and alarmingly, much of what he had read in Lord Alfred's letter was now starting to make sense.

"So, in a nutshell," said Matthew, as he came to the end of his unsavoury tale, "I was told to figure out some way of wheedling the Willoughby fortune away from you and pass pretty much all of it to him. If I didn't, my parole would be terminated and in no time I'd find myself back behind bars to face the wrath of the Boss."

Charles endeavoured to assimilate this disturbing news, in an ensuing silence which lasted a long time. From where Matthew sat, it appeared that Charles had lapsed into some sort of trance.

"Charles?" he asked, eventually, "Are you all right?"

The question seemed to bring Charles back into the here and now. He looked up at Matthew, then both breathed in and exhaled deeply.

"I appreciate your candour," he said, "but may I ask why you have told me all this? Why did you not simply try to invent some story which would play on my sympathy, and obtain the money you needed that way? You never know, it might've worked."

Matthew shrugged and shook his head.

"The amount I would've had to ask for was simply too high," he said. "No disrespect, Charles, but there is no way you would've just handed over the amount I needed. Also, I'm not the same man who went into prison all those years ago," he said. "I want to put the past behind me."

There was another silence, as Charles eyed his visitor, keenly. Was this really the same Matthew with whom he had had a near fatal altercation all those years ago? Had he changed? Had he, really? Was it safe to trust him? So far, at least, he did appear to be being disarmingly honest and open about the situation.

Matthew spoke again.

"After the Boss spoke to me and made his demands I gave this a lot of thought."

"I don't wonder at it."

"I must confess that I did consider a number of different ways in which I might achieve what the Boss wanted, all of which were less than honest. I even thought about just disappearing – falling off the grid and going underground. I knew that was a stupid option, though. If I'd done that I know I would've been looking over my shoulder for the rest of my life. I could never have slept peacefully again knowing that, sooner or later, he would track me down. The Boss has a long memory. In the end, though, there were three things which led to my decision to put everything on the table for you. Firstly, despite what you hear about prison not being effective, I really learnt my lesson in there, Charles. Honesty really is the best policy – I see that now – and also....''

His voice trailed off for a moment as he considered his next words.

"Also, I just couldn't square it with my conscience to be dictated to by that thug. I know that I had my differences with Dad, but even if he was a blackmailer, I'm determined not to become yet another victim of it – and especially not at the hands of someone like the Boss. There has to be a better way."

Charles nodded.

"And...? You said there were three things."

"Yes. To be frank with you, I still feel so guilty about what happened before and I want to make it up to you. The fact is, the Boss is a nasty piece of work. He has an extensive network of contacts, and if I hadn't agreed to help him I know he would've found someone else who would. Once he heard about Dad's fortune, and how he came by it, and that it had now all passed to you, it was only going to be a matter of time before he came sniffing around. I thought that if I warned you about the attention you were attracting, you would have time to think about how to handle it, and – ''

He hesitated for a moment before continuing.

"… and if I could help you in any way I'd be glad to do it."

There was another pause as Charles considered. His gaze was focused on the two cups on the table, both of which were still virtually full, but whose contents had been forgotten and had gone cold. The whole atmosphere suddenly felt stark and bleak. Even the sparrows had ceased their cheerful singing.

"Do you have any idea," Charles said, eventually breaking the silence, "as to what size my so-called fortune is?"

Matthew's eyes widened.

"Now that you mention it, no, not really. I only know that it must be pretty substantial."

"Wrong. It *was* pretty substantial, but the passage of time and the enormous expenses involved in keeping a place like this going have taken their toll."

"What are you saying? Is there nothing left?" Matthew suddenly appeared anxious.

Charles chuckled.

"Oh, nothing so dramatic! There is still plenty to sustain a comfortable living, but over the years a sizeable slice has disappeared. What remains is, I suspect, nowhere near the level of unimaginable wealth that people perceive." Charles leant his head back in his chair and sighed. "Oh, Matthew," he continued, "at first, I had such great plans for this place. I spent a lot on trying to renovate the house, and I even commissioned feasibility studies to see how things could be improved." He paused before adding, "but when I was told that the ocean was slowly eroding the cliffs it seemed silly to pursue any major works. That's why so much of the house is in a state of disrepair now."

"Do you know how long it will be before the ocean does its worst?" asked Matthew. "Is the house really doomed?"

Charles threw his hands in the air.

"Ha! There's the irony," he said. "It may never happen at all. It's a possibility; not a certainty. Anyway, all this is beside the point. The point is that there is nowhere near as much money sloshing around as there once was."

"I hear you," said Matthew, "but here's the thing: although the Boss seems to know a great deal, I don't think he'll be aware that the fortune has diminished to such an extent. Even if he does work it out, I suspect he'll still feel that there is bound to be enough to justify all the effort needed to get hold of it."

"So you think it inevitable that he's going to pay me a visit?"

"Not him personally, of course, but you can be certain that whoever comes on his behalf will not be the sort of person you would want to invite round for afternoon tea."

"Suppose I were to accept your offer of help," said Charles, "and that by working together we somehow managed to keep the remains of the fortune where it belongs, what then? What will you do? This Boss that you have mentioned is hardly going to be pleased with you, is he? I agree with you that he's not just going to forget about it."

"Well…," Matthew began, and cleared his throat, "this is the part where I put myself at your mercy. As I mentioned, one of my options was to simply disappear. Being realistic, in the end I think that's probably what I'll still need to do. However, and speaking candidly, I would have a far greater chance of success if I had a little capital behind me. Before having this conversation I was hoping you might be able to assist me, so that I wouldn't have to seek help from less reputable persons. Now, though, it sounds as if that may not be possible after all."

Charles let out a long, slow sigh.

"Matthew," he said, "I assure you there is no issue there. Of course I could help you – to an extent, at least. However, I'm just a solicitor. All my life I've worked in an office. Show me a contract or an official document of some sort and I'm in my element, but all this talk of blackmail and thugs is not my area of expertise at all."

Matthew gave a wry smile.

"Believe it or not," he said, "that fact had not escaped my

attention, but don't be so self-effacing. You're far more than being just a regular office worker. I know you're a financial wizard. So, here is my idea: I think I could spin a line which would keep the Boss and his associate at bay for a little while. This would give you the time to put arrangements in place which would stop him getting his hands on the money. Once this is all over, if you would be willing to give me a helping hand so I could get back on my feet, I promise I'll be out of your way and will not trouble you any further."

"Hmm… but once your delaying tactic has run its course and the Boss finally comes calling, he won't be best pleased when he finds all the money has gone."

"True. Therefore, although the thought of this does stick in my throat, I suggest that you arrange for a certain sum to be made available for him – an amount which is enough to convince him that I have done what he asked, but not enough to seriously damage your assets. We need him to think that he has bled you dry, so that he won't come back again in the future."

Charles considered this.

"I daresay I probably could conceal most of it in places where even someone as devious as the Boss wouldn't think to look for it," he said. "However, before we begin to talk about that, although you came to bring me this unsettling news, I think I may have some news for you, too."

"You have news – for me?"

"I think so, yes. Come with me."

Charles stood up and walked back into the house, with Matthew following along behind, wondering what this news could possibly be.

CHAPTER 7

The cellar beneath Heston Lodge was much larger than it at first appeared, yet it was illuminated by nothing more than a single naked light bulb which hung from the low cobwebbed ceiling. Several of the numerous packing cases which it housed had already been opened, their contents strewn around the on stone-flagged floor.

There was nowhere near enough light to be absolutely certain that the search was being conducted efficiently, but Meg had been adamant that there was no room upstairs for anything to be brought up from below. So Kristin had to hunt in the semi-gloom, swearing and cursing under her breath, as yet another of the old cases yielded nothing of interest. If this search proved unfruitful, next time she would bring a torch, she thought to herself.

What *could* be ascertained, despite the poor lighting, was that most of the cases contained nothing but junk! True, there were occasional items which may have held sentimental value – a number of old framed photographs had emerged, for instance – but much of the rest was pointless clutter. Why would anyone want to hold on to all these old utility bills? What was the point of keeping saucepans with broken handles or threadbare soft toys? One wooden case was found to contain a stack of old blankets, where the dampness of the atmosphere had managed to creep down the inside and spread to the fabric, creating an ugly smell of mildew and spread of mould.

Every so often, as yet another lid was prised open, it would create a current in the damp air which sent the light bulb swinging back and forth on its grimy flex, causing shadows to move up and down on the walls, adding further inconvenience to the search.

"How's it all going?" came a cheerful voice from the top of the cellar steps. "Are you ready for another cup of tea yet?"

"No thanks, Meg," Kristin called from below, trying to emulate the happy-sounding voice above, though without success.

"I have some cake as well, if you would like?"

"No!" and then, more softly, "No, thank you."

"I thought you said you were going to bring James with you to help?"

In the semi-darkness, Kristin grimaced and rolled her eyes.

"I know, Meg. I did ask him, but unfortunately he is very busy just now. He'll try to come next time."

"Oh. I was so hoping to see him. I've made him some flapjacks. He loves those."

"If you'd like to wrap some up I'll give them to him when I see him."

"Oh, would you? That is really most kind. Shan't be a moment then."

The sound of the elderly footsteps could be heard retreating across the creaking floorboards, heading for the kitchen, allowing Kristin to resume concentration on her search once again.

"Stupid old biddy," she whispered, as she began to rummage, roughly and noisily, through yet another case of worthless memorabilia.

***

"Take a look at this."

Charles and Matthew had crossed the rickety bridge and now stood inside the octagonal tower. Matthew reached out and took the cream coloured envelope which was being offered to him.

"What is it?"

"I wish I knew."

Matthew removed the sheet of paper from within and read the four typed words.

We know your secret.

Matthew's face bore a solemn expression as Charles spoke again.

"At first, I thought that perhaps someone was having a joke, playing some sort of mischievous prank. Things like this have occasionally happened before."

Matthew glanced up.

"Really?" he said.

"Oh, it was never anything serious. I always put it down to local kids just messing around and then I'd forget about it. For some reason, though, my instinct was telling me that this time things were a bit more serious. Then this arrived."

As he spoke he handed over the second message which Matthew opened, quickly.

We haven't forgotten.

We are watching you.

"Hmm. This is worse than I thought," said Matthew. "The Boss told me that one of his associates would be in touch, but I had assumed they would contact me only."

"What are you saying?" Charles asked.

"It would appear that these associates have decided to embark on a course of intimidation too."

Charles felt his pulse quicken.

"What should I do? Do you think I should call the police?"

Matthew shook his head.

"Until a crime has actually been committed there is nothing the police could do," he said. "In any case, so far we don't even know who these people are."

"But surely an officer could be placed on guard duty, or something, in case they try to deliver another message?"

"For how long? And how many officers would be needed to effectively keep watch over all the comings and goings on an estate the size of Heston?"

"So we just sit back and do nothing?"

"Not necessarily." Matthew looked down again at the unfolded sheets of paper in his hand. "What do these messages mean? In particular, what is this secret they are referring to in the first message?"

"I really don't know, but I am increasingly feeling as though I ought to."

"What do you mean by that?"

Charles crossed to the desk in the centre of the room and opened one of its drawers."

"Let me show you something I came across a few days ago," he said.

Reaching into the drawer, Charles pulled out a beige coloured notebook. He indicated the pages where Lord Alfred's letter and the poem were written and handed the book to Matthew, who quickly skimmed through them. As he did so, his face became increasingly incredulous with every passing moment.

"Not another ruddy treasure hunt," he moaned. "What on earth is he talking about this time?"

"I've no idea. Frankly, I just don't know what to make of it," said Charles. "All I can think is that Lord Alfred appears to have been aware of the likelihood that people were going to come looking for him in pursuit of some financial gain, and it sounds like he's hidden a secret stash somewhere to be used to pay them off."

"So where is it?"

"Goodness only knows." Charles gestured at the notebook as he spoke. "Apparently, that poem holds the answer."

Matthew groaned.

"I haven't forgotten what a ruddy rigmarole it was the first time," he said. "I don't think I can face going through all that again."

"You and me both, but I don't think it's our task to do so."

"What? What are you talking about?"

"Well, look." Charles took the letter and pointed, reading out loud. *"If you are the right person to solve this little conundrum, you will know how to do it.* There. Since neither of us knows how to solve it, it follows that neither of us is the right person."

Matthew shrugged.

"If you're right, that gets us off the hook in one sense, but I don't think pleading innocence is a strategy that's going to satisfy the Boss. Sooner or later, his associates are going to come calling, and it's clear from their messages that they believe you to be the holder of an important secret."

"Are you suggesting that this… this *Boss* thinks that I know where Lord Alfred hid his secret hoard?"

Matthew shook his head.

"No, I don't think so," he said. "Given that you only

found out about this hidden store very recently, it is unlikely that anyone else knows about it either – not even the Boss. I suspect that the secret which these messages refer to is the fact that Dad was blackmailing a large number of people."

Charles rubbed his eyes.

"I fear," he said, "that the amount of money remaining in the Willoughby coffers will fall far below the expectations of this Boss character."

"If that's the case, he won't be pleased."

"If there was *some* way we could solve the enigma of this blasted poem," said Charles, gesturing at the notebook which still lay open on the desk, "perhaps the amount that would be forthcoming from this secret hoard would be enough to pacify him."

"Maybe, but there's no way of knowing until we find out how much is there."

"OK, but how do we do that? The letter seems to be saying that there is only one person who can solve this puzzle."

"Yes, but since we don't know who that person is, perhaps we should at least give it a try ourselves? After all, we didn't do too badly last time, did we?"

Charles sighed again, suddenly realising he'd been doing a lot of sighing lately.

"To tell you the truth, I'm not sure I have the stomach for it," he said, "but in the absence of any other ideas I suppose it would do no harm to at least give it a try."

"OK," said Matthew. "Shall we get started then?"

"Just one thing, though," said Charles. "Assuming that we do manage to solve this problem, since we have no idea how much we might find, I cannot guarantee that I'll be able to provide you with the capital you're hoping for, in return for your help."

Matthew nodded.

"Understood," he said, "but Dad was a shrewd old codger. I'm sure that whatever is waiting at the end of this trail will be worth hunting for."

"I suppose you're right," replied Charles. "Well, in that case, might I suggest that we take this letter and poem down to the drawing room? It's far more comfortable there, and James can bring us some of Mrs Gillcarey's delicious cake while we ponder."

Matthew smiled.

"There, you see!" he exclaimed. "We're making progress already."

Carrying the notebook with its enigmatic contents, they left the octagonal room and began to cross the rickety bridge, making their way back towards the main house.

***

Below stairs, in the meticulously tidy kitchen, James watched as Mrs Gillcarey carefully lifted a freshly baked bread pudding, still hot from the oven, from its earthenware dish and transferred it to a large serving platter.

"Now then, Mr James," she said, "don't you start any of your moaning. I know Mr Seymour asked for cake, but this bread pudding is all fresh and ready. Once I've added a dollop of cream both he and master Matthew will love it."

James did not reply but gave a slight smile. Mrs Gillcarey's gastronomic creations never failed to impress, and this pudding was no exception. Topped with nutmeg and cinnamon, and infused with plump, juicy sultanas, the mere sight of it, with a huge plume of steam issuing forth, was enough to set even the driest mouth-watering.

"Anyway," she added, "how is Mr Seymour getting on with master Matthew? Is everything going along all right?"

"The conversation appears to be quite amicable," said

James, nodding. "Surprising really, when you think about all that happened…."

His voice tailed off. Mrs Gillcarey placed the bread pudding on a tray, together with a small jug of cream, before adding a fresh pot of Darjeeling tea alongside. Standing back, she surveyed the whole ensemble, gave a little grunt of satisfaction and indicated that James could now take it.

When he didn't move, she raised her eyebrows.

"Well? Pick it up, James. Don't want it to get all cold, now do we?"

"Oh, I'm sorry," he said. "I was miles away."

He leant forward and was about to pick up the tray, but paused when Mrs Gillcarey spoke again.

"So I could see. Something bothering you then?"

"No, not really. It's just that when Mr Seymour asked me for the cake I overheard a snatch of his conversation with master Matthew. It sounds as though they may have stumbled across another of Lord Alfred's riddles."

Mrs Gillcarey threw her hands in the air.

"Oh, Lord help us!" she said. "Not another one! Do you remember the first time, when they would suddenly go running off to solve some clue or other? Do you know how many of my dinners were left half finished?"

"Ah, dear Mrs Gillcarey," said James, "you shouldn't take it so personally. I think I know Mr Seymour deeply appreciates all your efforts in the kitchen." He then took her hand and raised it to his lips. "As do I," he said.

"Ooh, get along with you now," she replied, with a quiet giggle and gently pushing him away. "You'll make me blush, you will."

∗∗∗

"Did you find what you were looking for?"

Meg smiled sweetly as Kristin, who was disgruntled, dishevelled and dusty, clambered and limped her way back up the steps from the cellar.

"Sadly, no, but I know that journal must be around here somewhere so I suppose I'll just have to keep searching until I find it."

"Well, if it's not in the cellar, I'm sure I have no idea where it might be. Have you asked James? I'm sure he will know. I think he's coming soon. Did you remember to ask him?"

"Yes, I asked him," Kristin lied, "and he said he would come as soon as he could."

"Oh, thank you. You are really very kind," said Meg. Then she added, "Do be kind to James – did I mention he has Alzheimer's?"

Kristin responded with a curt nod and half a smile.

"I'll keep it in mind," she said. "Well, I'd best be going. I'll see you again soon."

As she was loping towards the door, Meg called after her.

"I suppose it's possible that this journal you keep talking about might be somewhere in the main house instead. Had you thought of that?"

Kristin suppressed a scream of frustration, and forced herself to maintain a sweet tone.

"Yes, I had thought of that, but you told me it was in your cellar."

"Oh, did I? Perhaps I did. Perhaps it is. When you get to my age, you can't always remember things clearly, you know."

Kristin managed to turn away before rolling her eyes yet again.

"Time for me to go," she said. "Thanks for your help."

"Oh, would you like to take a slice of –"

The door slammed.

"– cake?"

Meg stood, quietly and alone, regarding the closed door. "Ah well, maybe next time," she said. "I'll make some for James too."

The door to the cellar was still ajar and, as she passed by, Meg glanced down the steps. What she saw made her cry out in surprise. Case after case had been torn open, and the contents, strewn hither and thither, now littered the floor.

"Oh, dear!" she cried. "Oh, dear! How could I have allowed things to become so messy? Ooh, I hope that nice lady didn't notice any of this. Think what she would say! Oh, oh dear. Whatever am I to do? I can't clear all this away by myself. I don't know where it all goes. When James comes I'll ask him to help me tidy up. Then everything will be all right again. Yes, that's the way." She moved through into the kitchen. "Now," she said, "I think it's time for some tea. I wonder where I put it. Oh… did I remember to buy some?"

CHAPTER 8

A tray, laden with hot tea, steaming bread pudding and thick dairy cream had been wheeled into the drawing room on an ornate brass trolley. However, despite the appearance and the aroma, both of which were most attractive, they remained untouched, at least for now.

The book containing the poem, written in Lord Alfred Willoughby's distinctive handwriting, lay open on the table. Matthew was scrutinising it carefully, while Charles paced about the room, deep in thought.

"The sun bleached stone," said Matthew. "If I remember correctly, didn't the original poem also mention that?"

"Correct, and that is what led us to the family cemetery and the eventual discovery of the crypt."

"Have you been to take a look at it?"

"No."

"Why not?"

"According to the letter, if I was the right person to solve the mystery I would already know how to do it but, since I don't know how, I assumed that wandering aimlessly around some old tombs would prove fruitless."

"Point taken. Still, it might be worth taking a look anyway. Something useful might present itself. You never know."

"Here's a thought," said Charles, from across the room. "The poem mentions an acacia tree, doesn't it?"

Matthew glanced down at the words again.

"Yes, it does," he said.

Charles walked over to Matthew and, taking the book from him, read the poem yet again.

"I had always thought that all the trees in the cemetery were cypresses," said Charles.

"So…?"

"Well, I haven't actually set foot in the cemetery for ages, so this is just a stab in the dark, but might there be an acacia tree in there too? If there is, perhaps that might lead to a further clue?"

"I suppose it wouldn't do any harm to at least go and see. Do you know what an acacia tree looks like, though? I don't think I do."

Just then, there was the sound of a door opening. Charles and Matthew glanced up as Kristin came limping in, looking anything but happy. However, when she saw Matthew she managed to twist her distorted features into a smile and loped her way towards him.

"Hello," she said. "I don't believe we've met. Charles, aren't you going to introduce us?"

As soon as Kristin appeared, Charles had closed the notebook and slipped it into a drawer, hoping he had managed to do so discreetly.

"Oh, yes, of course, I'm sorry. Matthew, this is Kristin. Kristin, Matthew."

They shook hands, and Matthew made a good attempt at hiding his shock at Kristin's disfigured appearance.

"Kristin is… erm… a friend," said Charles.

"Oh, come along, Charles," said Kristin. "There's no

need to be coy. She looked straight at Matthew and said, "Charles and I were once engaged to be married."

Matthew's mouth fell open in surprise.

"But that was all a long time ago," Charles interjected.

"Ah… OK," Matthew stammered, not quite knowing what to say. "So… erm… what brings you here now?"

"I'm just visiting," she said, "but I'm also looking for somewhere new to live, so I'm trying to use this opportunity to discover what accommodation might be available in the area."

"But there isn't anything round here," Matthew said. "The nearest house is miles away."

"Quite. That's why I've been staying on site and running up my dear ex-fiancé's phone bill by calling up as many estate agents as I have been able to find." Then she glanced over at Charles. "Sorry about that, darling," she said.

Charles felt his face redden slightly at her words.

"So how has the house hunting been going?" he asked.

"Nothing so far," said Kristin, with a sigh, "but there's always tomorrow, isn't there? Honestly, today I made so many calls I felt as though the phone were glued to my ear, so I took a break and have been outside, walking in the grounds. It's really quite pleasant."

She then looked at Matthew. "And what about you?" she asked. "What's your connection here?"

"I'm the son of the late Lord Alfred Willoughby," said Matthew.

"Forgive me, I didn't realise I was in the presence of greatness," Kristin replied. Charles observed that she had spoken with a tinge of sarcasm. He hoped that Matthew hadn't noticed it.

"After my father died, Charles moved into Heston Grange and we stayed in touch."

"I see."

Charles realised he wanted to move away from this subject as quickly as possible, and came up with the perfect change of direction.

"Good gracious!" he said. "Look, the bread pudding has been standing here all this time. I'm sure Mrs Gillcarey will never forgive us if we let it go cold."

Without pausing to ask whether his half-brother or ex-fiancé wanted some, he placed slices onto plates and handed them over.

"Help yourselves to cream," he said.

Once the thick topping had been added, silence descended as the delicious slices of moist, succulent bread pudding were consumed. No sooner had Charles finished his last mouthful, he glanced out of the window, then turned to Matthew and spoke.

"It's starting to cloud over," he said. "If we're lucky, I might be able to show you that thing in the garden before the rain comes."

"Oh... erm... yes, good idea," said Matthew, setting his plate down.

"What thing are you talking about?" asked Kristin.

"Oh, nothing," said Charles. "Matthew is a keen horticulturalist and wanted to see the work our groundsman has been doing in the walled garden."

"I didn't even realise you had a walled garden."

"Oh, yes. It's just a bit further along from the maze."

"I didn't know you had one of those either."

"Ha! In that case, I must give you a guided tour at some point. Anyway, Matthew, shall we go? Kristin, do have another slice of bread pudding, if you like. Mrs Gillcarrey always hates it if we don't finish everything."

Before Kristin could say anything further, Charles and Matthew had left the room, the door closed and she was alone. She cast a glance at the remaining slices of bread pudding which did, indeed, look inviting, but found that she had something else on her mind.

As she'd entered the room, a few minutes earlier, she thought she had caught a glimpse of Charles swiftly putting something away... in that drawer, over there. She might have been wrong, but it almost looked as though he didn't want her to see what it was. In all likelihood it was nothing of any great importance, certainly nothing that would concern her.

And yet... what could it be?

With her curiosity aroused, Kristin limped across the room towards the closed drawer.

***

It had been years since Charles and Matthew had last stood together in this private cemetery. Back then, it was already unkempt and overgrown, but now it was even more so, such that they both had to take great care to avoid tripping over the web of thick, gnarled creepers which covered the ground.

The dense, high hedge surrounding the burial site still did a fine job of keeping the chilly wind at bay, and even the sound of the nearby crashing ocean waves was stilled in here, bringing an eerie serenity to this now disused resting place.

At the far end, there was the familiar large marble tomb, nestling beneath the overhanging branches of the large cypress tree. Now, though, it was smothered in ivy, with large, leathery leaves all but obscuring the white stonework beneath.

"Look over here!"

Charles looked round as Matthew called out to him, and began to carefully pick his way over the panoply of obstacles and trip hazards which threatened to throw him down with every step he took.

"What is it?" he asked, as he finally came alongside.

"Remember this?" said Matthew.

He pointed to the ground, where a flat gravestone lay embedded in the surrounding turf and other scrambled foliage.

"How could I forget?" Charles replied. "I suppose the passageway underneath will still be there."

He raised his foot and stamped firmly on the stone. Sure enough, the tell-tale hollow sound from below could be heard.

"Yes, it's there all right."

"I wonder if anyone has used it since then," said Matthew.

"I doubt it. Anyway, if they did, they did so without my permission. I could have them arrested for trespassing."

"Let's just hope we don't have to lift that blasted stone this time round. Once was quite enough, and it almost put my back out."

Matthew then looked round at the sorry-looking assortment of weather-beaten trees and plants, and sighed.

"Do any of these look like an acacia tree to you?" he asked.

"No idea," said Charles. "Anyway, I still can't shake from my mind what the letter said – that point about the right person understanding the poem and knowing what to do."

"That's very encouraging. I hope you haven't forgotten that at some point we are to be visited by some very unpleasant people?"

"Of course I haven't forgotten."

"Good. In that case, regardless of what the letter says, we need to try and solve this blasted puzzle as soon as possible."

"I agree, but I don't think we're going to achieve that by standing out here. Anyway, the temperature's dropping. I suggest we go back inside and take another look at the poem – and we can have another slice of bread pudding at the same time."

"Yes, unless little miss Whatsername has snaffled it all."

"Kristin," said Charles. "Her name's Kristin."

"Whatever."

As they began to make their way back towards the house, neither of them spotted the shadowy figure observing them from a distance. Hidden within a clump of trees, the black-clad form was virtually invisible. Once Charles and Matthew were at a sufficient distance, the figure quietly slipped away in the opposite direction.

***

As Charles and Matthew were re-entering the drawing room they almost bumped into James, who had just reached the door with the trolley as he wheeled away the remains of the bread pudding.

"Oh, do excuse me, sir. I had no wish to run you over."

"That's all right, James, but I will need to see your driving licence."

"Very droll, sir."

"Oh, you're taking the bread pudding away?"

"I assumed you'd finished, sir. Would you rather I left it with you?"

"Actually, we were looking forward to having a little more so, yes, please do leave it here – and perhaps you could bring us a fresh pot of tea?"

"Of course, sir. Right away."

James trundled the trolley back to its place, where he served two more slices of the delectable pudding before departing to fetch the requested tea.

As they both tucked in once again, it occurred to Charles that there was no sign of Kristin. She must have gone back to her room, he supposed. As he chewed his first mouthful, Charles realised he had forgotten to add cream; but, reaching for the small jug, he was disappointed to find that there was none left. He set his plate down and crossed the room to the drawer where he had recently placed Lord Alfred's journal. Taking it out, he first found the letter, then turned the page and re-read the poem once more, squinting to bring the spidery script into focus:

The Falchion points the way

Behind the tree lies a sun-bleached stone
Near or far, 'tis still called home
Ah! Ne'er more earnest was it meant
Hither and thither the boy was sent

Hoping! Yes, kept hope alive
Or sustained an outcome tragic
Trying to pursue acacia
Growing old with super ego

Nearly missed the old enigma
Latent not, away it went
Opened, then, fair fortune's window
Entered, there, a greater power

Upon reaching the end, he sighed. Whatever the answer to this mysterious puzzle might be, Lord Alfred had managed to disguise it with mastery. On the other hand, according to the accompanying letter, if the 'right person' were to read it, the answer would be obvious.

There, then.

Clearly, Charles was not the right person.

In that case, who was?

He lowered the book and rubbed his eyes. If it proved impossible to track down the mysterious individual, what was Charles supposed to say when the associates of this sinister Boss character came calling? And, in that case, where would Matthew fit in to all of this? What would happen to him if the enigma were not solved by then?

Looking across the room to where Matthew had almost finished devouring yet another slice of bread pudding, Charles quietly marvelled at the extraordinary pathways which had thrown the two of them together, not once but twice. Was Matthew such a bad character, really, he wondered, or was he just the product of an unfortunate past? Could it be that he really had changed for the better, as he now professed? Charles hoped so.

He was jolted from his thoughts by the sound of the door opening, which heralded the return of James with some fresh tea.

"I thought you might like some Assam this time, sir," he said, as he began to pour.

At that moment it suddenly occurred to Charles that he had been meaning to ask James about Lord Alfred's journal on several occasions but had been distracted each time. He would correct that right now.

"James," he said, "A few days ago I came across this in the tower. It appears to be some sort of journal and I'd been intending to show it to you. Did you know of its existence?"

James took the notebook and leafed through it.

"No, sir," he said, "I was not aware of it. Where did you find it?"

Charles told him about the secret compartment he had discovered in the bottom of the safe.

"I can't say I'm surprised," said James. "We know how much His Lordship enjoyed setting up these little mysteries."

"But the poem and the letter don't tell you anything?"

"I'm afraid not, sir, though my curiosity has certainly been aroused. I would love to know what he is referring to when he mentions a 'contingency plan'."

"Hmm. You and me both."

"Will that be all, sir?"

"Yes, thank you, James."

A few moments later, the door had closed, and Charles and Matthew were alone once again. The bread pudding was now finished. The flames in the hearth danced around merrily, and the steam rose from the freshly poured tea in a way which seemed homely and comforting. Yet, the two men did not have peace of mind. They had a problem to solve and knew that they did not have much time.

***

Mrs Gillcarey positively purred with pleasure as James returned to the kitchen and informed her that virtually every scrap of her legendary bread pudding was being readily consumed.

"It seems they're enjoying it then," she crowed.

"I think you may be right," said James.

"Have they made any progress with the latest mystery, or whatever it is?"

"Well, yes and no."

"Oh, now you're the one who's being all mysterious. Whatever do you mean?"

"It appears that Mr Seymour found a journal belonging to Lord Alfred, which had been hidden in a secret compartment. Among other things, the journal contains a letter and a poem, clearly handwritten by His Lordship. Mr Seymour allowed me to read them, but they made no sense to me at all. In fact, I fear that the hidden message, whatever it may be, is even more cleverly obscured than was the case on that previous occasion all those years ago."

"Well, if the two of them are going to be turning detective again I suppose I'd better get my thinking cap on to make sure they're well supplied with victuals. Can't expect them to think clearly on an empty stomach, now can we?"

At that moment, an idea suddenly surfaced from deep within James' subconscious mind and abruptly appeared at the front of his thoughts in full focus.

"Bless my soul," he whispered.

"What's that?" asked Mrs Gillcarey. "What did you say?"

"I think I need to go and speak to Mr Seymour, immediately," he said.

***

When Kristin first removed the journal from the drawer and realised what it contained, all thoughts of eating bread pudding instantly vanished, and her first thought was to take this beige coloured book straight back to her room.

But then she had a more sensible idea. After all, she did not want to arouse suspicions unnecessarily. In an adjacent drawer she had found some plain paper and a pencil. After reading the letter, she had then copied out the poem as quickly as her deformed body would allow, and had heaved a sigh of relief when she managed to complete the task before Charles and Matthew returned.

Now, back in her room once again, Kristin sat on her bed and stared at the sheet of paper in front of her, scrutinising it closely.

However, it was quickly becoming apparent that

whatever secret might be concealed within its lines it did not intend to give itself up easily. Kristin cursed under her breath.

"You should have taken better care of me, Charles Seymour," she whispered. "Yes, you should. If you had been more of a gentleman and treated me properly, like a lady, I wouldn't have felt the need to go looking elsewhere, and I wouldn't have ended up looking like this. It's all your fault. You've brought this on yourself and I intend to get what should rightfully be mine."

All other thoughts then faded from her mind, as she focused on the poem in front of her, giving it her fullest concentration.

***

Matthew and Charles were shoulder to shoulder, leaning over the poem which they had placed on a desk by the window.

"Do you think the line that says *'growing old with super ego'* is a reference to dad himself?" Matthew suggested.

"Ha! I suppose it's possible. He did indeed have quite a large ego."

"Ain't that the truth."

"But I'm not sure he would have ever admitted, even to himself, that his was a *super* ego. I suspect he probably preferred to think of himself as being quite humble."

Matthew snorted.

"Yeah, right," he said.

There was a polite knock at the door and James entered. Before any word was spoken, Charles noticed that he appeared to be lacking something of his usual poise, and seemed to be a little flustered.

"I'm sorry to disturb you, sir," he said.

"Not at all, James. What is it?"

"Sir, forgive me if I seem a little impertinent, but may I take another look at Lord Alfred's poem?"

"Yes. Yes, of course."

Charles lifted the journal from the desk and handed it to James, who regarded it, keenly, while Charles and Matthew both looked on. After a few moments, James gave a quiet murmur of satisfaction and handed the book back.

"Well?" Charles asked. "Have you noticed something in the poem?"

"Sir," said James, "in his letter, Lord Alfred mentions that only the right person would know how to solve this puzzle."

"That's correct, yes."

There was a short pause before James spoke again.

"Well, sir, I have a suspicion that the 'right person' might be me.

CHAPTER 9

In the prison, the cell occupied by the Boss was, at his request, the one at the end of the corridor. He had selected this one particularly because its location afforded him a modicum of extra privacy, over and above that experienced by the other inmates, as well as it being slightly larger than the others.

The unwritten agreement which the Boss had with the prison governor and the officers, by which he would keep this bunch of otherwise unruly inmates in order, did bring with it certain privileges. While most other cells had only a bed, his cell had also been equipped with a desk and chair; and it was not just any old chair, but a *swivel* chair. This detail was important: the fact that he could rotate himself in either direction made his cell feel, to him, less like a cell and more like an office – a fact which he liked, since whenever it became necessary to summon other inmates, either to issue instructions or a reprimand, it gave the whole meeting a more formal, official feeling.

When meals were distributed, he was always given a portion which was larger than normal, though the other prisoners were unaware of this. He was also allowed to have a folding screen which could be positioned such that he could use the toilet in his cell without being viewed through the peephole in the cell door.

And … he received his mail unread and uncensored.

The fact that he had been able to secure this last privilege was a significant coup. It meant that he was still able to control his extensive network of operations beyond the prison walls, and be kept fully informed of all developments by his band of henchmen who had, so far, shown themselves to be completely loyal and reliable.

Of course, the Boss was not naïve. The fact that his squad of helpers were at liberty on the outside while he was incarcerated inside was less than ideal, and he could think of certain individuals who might try to wrestle his empire away from him, given the chance.

But the wily Boss had been sure to put arrangements in place so that even if such a usurping were to be attempted, he was confident that it could be managed successfully and its perpetrators dealt with swiftly.

For now, though, everything seemed to be sailing along nicely, on an even keel.

Good.

And now, as he sat in his personal chair, in his spacious cell, and read his latest item of mail, a smug smile of satisfaction etched itself onto his broad, pock-marked face.

Contact has been made. Progress appears to be good. You will be updated regularly.

The Boss put his hands behind his head, leant back in his swivel chair and spun himself round, at a thoughtful, sedate speed.

Soon, he thought to himself, soon the Willoughby fortune will be in my grasp.

***

"What do you mean?" Matthew asked, an incredulous tone creeping into his voice. "How can you be the right person?"

"I do realise that it might seem a little unlikely," James replied, "but after I saw the poem and went back down to the kitchen, a small detail – something which happened years ago, and which I had all but forgotten – suddenly returned to my mind."

"Please tell us," said Charles. "So far, we've drawn a complete blank, so if you can shed any light on this mystery it would really be most helpful."

"Well, sir," said James, "it happened one evening, shortly before Lord Alfred's sad demise. I took him his usual glass of sherry and found him at his desk poring over many official-looking documents and a large pile of correspondence which looked quite daunting. I didn't pay too much attention but, as I set the drink down, His Lordship spoke to me. He told me that when the time came, he would like me to read his first and last letters."

"And you think that time has now come?" asked Charles.

James nodded. "I believe so," he said.

Charles gasped, in exasperation. "But he wrote a great many," he said. "I've been gradually working my way through all his personal correspondence and effects, and it's an endless task. It has taken me, literally, years, and the end is still nowhere in sight. How are we to know whether he was referring to letters he had written and sent to other people, or letters which he had received? And which would be his last letter anyway? Would it have been the latest one at the time he spoke to you, or perhaps one which he wrote subsequently? And where are they now? How are we to find them? Oh, this is all too complicated."

James waited patiently, until Charles finished speaking.

"May I continue, sir?" he asked, politely.

"Yes, of course. I'm sorry. Please proceed."

"Thank you, sir. Naturally, I did not press His Lordship for anything beyond what he had decided to say – that would not have been appropriate. I was, however, a little bold in asking him what he meant by 'when the time came'. He simply said that when the moment arrived I would recognise it. In this, it turns out that Lord Alfred was taking a risk, since the moment has indeed come and, at first, I am ashamed to say I did not recognise it. However, now that I see the poem again, I think I can safely say that I do know the way to proceed – that is, I know the first step, at least."

He paused, while his audience of two watched him, captivated. Eventually, it was Matthew who broke the silence.

"So… what is the first step?" he asked.

"Allow me to fetch a sheet of paper," said James. He crossed the room and pulled out a notepad from a drawer. He then took a pencil from his inside pocket and picked up the journal.

"May I sit?" he asked.

"Of course."

James seated himself at the desk with the open journal and the notepad in front of him.

"When Lord Alfred spoke of his first and last letters," he began, "he was not referring to his correspondence at all. Rather, he was talking about the first and last letters of each line in this poem."

With that, James began to write. Charles and Matthew craned their necks to see, but James' handwriting was very small.

"So, first we have B," said James, as he wrote. "Then the last letter of that line is E. Then the first letter of the next line is N….”

He continued in like manner until, after an appreciable number of moments, he put the pencil down.

“It would appear that my suspicion was correct,” he said.

He leaned back in the chair and handed the sheet of paper to the two eager watchers.

It read: *Beneath the octagonal tower.*

“The crafty old bugger,” breathed Matthew. “He always liked his puzzles. How could we read the poem so many times and never spot something so obvious?”

“That’s because neither you nor I were the right person,” said Charles. “We looked at the poem but we didn’t see, because we didn’t know what we were looking for. Dear James, on the other hand, –” As he spoke he clapped a hand on the butler’s shoulder. “– James *is* the right person, so now progress has been made.”

“So,” said Matthew, “there is, apparently, something *under* the tower that we ought to go and find?”

“It would seem so,” said Charles. “James, would you please accompany us? Whether you realise it or not, it may well be that you have further knowledge which will prove just as invaluable.”

“Of course, sir. Shall I clear away the tea things first?” James indicated the half-empty cups and the now cold teapot. “It would be dreadfully untidy to leave them sitting there like that.”

“Actually, on this occasion I think that can wait,” said Charles.

“As you wish, sir.”

***

A few minutes later found the trio of Charles, Matthew and James outdoors and walking round the base of the octagonal tower, searching for – what? None of them really knew. Matthew scampered about like an excited puppy; Charles went with a little more poise, while James shuffled his way along quite slowly.

After they had done a complete circuit of the tower they stopped.

"There's no way in," Matthew lamented.

"We already knew that," said Charles. "We need to be looking for something else – something unusual, something out of the ordinary."

They all stood back and looked up at the defiant structure. It was indeed most unusual. Apart from its unorthodox shape, and its bizarre means of entry at second floor level, its style and design made it seem somewhat incongruous and rather out of keeping with the rest of the house. Whilst the main part of Heston Grange and this tower were both very old, the tower had clearly been built of a different stone and seemed to be slightly newer.

With the sound of the nearby waves crashing against the cliffs, the three men stood, gazing up at the imposing octagonal edifice. It almost seemed as though, by the simple act of staring, they hoped to persuade it to reveal an entrance which had been hitherto unnoticed.

Yet the tower remained resolutely silent.

"Perhaps there will be an underground entrance," Charles suggested. "Maybe there's a passageway that forms part of the network of tunnels that extends to the cliffs."

"That is a distinct possibility, sir," said James, "but, if that is the case, I fear we shall have our work cut out to find it. As you know, there are a great many tunnels in this area. To the best of my knowledge, they have never been fully explored, though we do know there are numerous entrances to them. It would be a huge task were we to try and navigate our way through them all."

"Then what the blazes are we supposed to do?" Matthew exploded, instantly regretting both the volume and tone of his voice. "Sorry," he said, a little more quietly.

"I can't help feeling," James continued, "that, given the apparent seriousness of the circumstances surrounding this particular puzzle, His Lordship would have enabled its solution to be identified a little more... directly."

"What do you mean?" asked Charles.

"This may be irrelevant," James replied, "but, as you can see, the only apparent means of access to the tower is by that bridge up there." As he spoke, he pointed upward towards the swaying structure, which, Charles thought, somehow seemed even more rickety today than usual. "Notice that the entrance is at second floor level," James continued. "Over the years, I would occasionally wonder whether there might be anything beneath that second floor room, but I didn't ever have cause to give the idea any serious consideration, until now."

What James said gave Charles real pause for thought, and he considered. Here was a tower, with its only apparent entrance way above the ground, while the levels beneath seemed to have no access at all. Why had he never thought about this before? It was unlikely that the lower levels would be solid. Surely, there must be some sort of space within? Given that they now had Lord Alfred's indication that there was something beneath the tower, this did seem very likely.

"If we are unable to find a way in from beneath," said Charles, thinking aloud, "are you suggesting that we might need to gain access from above – from the octagonal room itself?"

"I really don't know, sir. I mention it merely as a possibility."

"Then why are we still standing around out here?" Matthew piped up. "Let's get up there and start searching."

***

Not far away, concealed in a clump of trees, two silent figures using binoculars watched as Charles, Matthew and James walked around the base of the tower. They were too far away to hear what was being said, but once it became obvious that the trio was heading back into the house, they turned and slipped away through the trees, like fleeting shadows.

***

It was definitely the walled garden, said Kristin to herself. That was where Charles and Matthew had said they were going.

After sitting in her room and scrutinising the copied-out poem for quite some time, but without making any progress, a rising frustration had led Kristin to the notion that perhaps a visit to the walled garden might furnish her with some of the information she needed. Since the grounds were extensive, it had taken her some time to find its location but, at length, she did manage to reach her goal. Having first discovered the location of the maze, she then found that the walled garden was just beyond it, as Charles had said in their earlier conversation.

However, as she hobbled, painfully, through the entrance, the site that greeted her was not encouraging.

She had heard Charles say that he wanted to show Matthew the recent work which had been done on it – but, in fact, the place was a mess. Although it bore the appearance of having been well tended at some point in the past, now it lay barren and desolate. It was clear that no work had been done here for some considerable time. It was a mass of weeds and stones, with not a single flower anywhere to be seen.

Why had Charles lied to her?

And what was her best course of action now?

With a snarl, she heaved her deformed body around and began to stomp her way back towards the house.

✳✳✳

Being no longer sufficiently sure of foot to tackle the challenges of the rickety bridge, James had remained in the main house, while Charles and Matthew had crossed over into the octagonal tower once again.

The two of them now stood there, in the dim light of the oil lamp, surveying the room as best they could.

"Why did Dad never think to install electricity in here?" he moaned.

"Certainly, at this point, a little more illumination would have been helpful," Charles agreed.

In the centre of the room sat Lord Alfred's impressive desk. Around the edges of the room, five of the eight walls were lined with filing cabinets, while two of the others each housed a safe, one of which contained the secret compartment which had turned out to be the hiding place for His Lordship's journal. Against the final wall was the small table, bearing the selection of old photos. As always, on the wall above, the clock devoutly ticked the seconds away, next to the ceremonial sword which hung alongside. The scabbard was showing signs of mildew now, and Charles wondered whether the weapon within had begun to rust away too – but that little discovery could wait.

"If there is a way into the base of the tower from here," said Matthew, "there must be some sort of trapdoor or something."

"Possibly. So where is it?"

Looking round, there was no obvious answer to that question. A simple process of deduction yielded the only plausible solution.

"It must be under one of these filing cabinets or safes," said Charles.

"Typical. Last time we had to almost break our backs raising that stone slab in the cemetery, and now we have to start carting this lot around!" Matthew gestured as he spoke.

Charles felt something of a sinking feeling. Certainly, none of the cabinets looked to be particularly light – and certainly not the safes – and, if indeed there was something waiting to be discovered underneath one of them, it was anyone's guess as to which one it might be.

"I suppose it's just a case of trial and error," said Charles. He then pointed to one of the filing cabinets at random. "Shall we start with this one?"

Matthew shrugged and sighed.

"I suppose so," he said.

They positioned themselves on opposite sides of the heavy metal repository.

"There's nothing to hold it by," Matthew groaned.

"We'll just have to try as best we can. Ready?"

Matthew nodded.

"Right, then. One... two... three!"

They bent their knees, grabbed the edges and lifted. The cabinet was so heavy that they managed to raise it only very slightly, but they somehow managed to shuffle their way across the floor with it for a short distance before letting the burden fall again, which it did with a loud thud.

The floor where the cabinet had stood was precisely that – a piece of floor, nothing more. There was no sign of any trapdoor or any other indication that anything awaited discovery beneath.

"That was fun," said Matthew, breathing heavily.

The act of lifting had sapped Charles of so much energy that he couldn't speak at all. Instead, he crouched on the floor, gasping, and taking in huge gulps of air. Other than the sounds of the two men breathing, the room was silent. It was in this silence that a faint sound began to be heard.

"Do you hear something?" Charles asked.

Matthew looked up and listened. There was something, and it sounded like a voice. Charles stood up and crossed to the door. He opened it and looked across the rickety bridge. James had opened the door on the other side and was calling to him.

"Sir! Sir!"

"Yes, James, what is it?"

"I think I may have some further information for you."

The wind was blowing in gusts, snatching away some of his words, so Charles crossed the swaying bridge to hear him more clearly.

"I'm sorry to bother you, sir," said James, once Charles had reached the other side, "but the title of Lord Alfred's poem was playing on my mind. I wasn't sure what a falchion was. I knew I had heard the word somewhere, but I couldn't quite place it. So I went down to the library and consulted a dictionary."

"Yes, and…?"

"A falchion is a type of sword, sir. Now, it has been quite a while since I was last able to cross the bridge, but I seem to remember that there is some sort of sword hanging on the wall. Did you happen to notice if it is still there?"

"Why, yes. Yes, it is."

"Well, sir, the title of the poem said that a falchion points the way. Knowing how much His Lordship loved his subtle clues, do you think my discovery might prove useful?"

Charles smiled.

"It may well do so!" he said, clapping his hands. "Thank

you, James."

"You are most welcome, sir."

Charles all but sprinted back across the undulating bridge to where Matthew was waiting.

"What did James have to say?" he asked.

Without a word, Charles walked straight to where the ceremonial sword hung on the wall. Sure enough, it was not hanging vertically, but had been strung at an angle, causing its tip to point towards the cabinet on the right.

"I suspect this is the one we need to shift," he said.

"How can you be so sure?"

"Oh, just a lucky hunch. Shall we?"

Matthew sighed and came to stand by the cabinet.

"Come on then. Let's do it."

With much heaving, grunting and scraping, the weighty filing cabinet was finally shifted to one side. The exhaustion which both men felt at their exertions was quickly forgotten, however, as they now beheld a trapdoor set into the floor.

"Eureka!" Matthew exclaimed.

Without a moment's hesitation, he dropped to his knees and grabbed at the metal ring in the door's surface.

"Be careful," Charles warned. "The wood might be rotten."

Cautiously, Matthew began to pull. Slowly, the door began to lift. As the dim light of the upper room began to penetrate into the opening aperture, Charles and Matthew gasped at what they saw.

A narrow, wrought iron spiral staircase could be seen descending into the darkness beneath.

Matthew looked at Charles and grinned.

"Just like old times, eh? Would you like to go first?"

"Oh, after you."

"We don't know how strong the stairs are, so it's probably best if we go down one at a time."

"Agreed. Be careful."

As Charles looked on, Matthew grasped the thin handrail and began, slowly and cautiously, to negotiate the narrow, twisting steps. After a few moments, he was swallowed up by the darkness.

"Are you all right?" Charles called down to him.

"Oh, never happier," came the reply. "I reckon I must be down to about the level of the first floor."

After a few more moments, Matthew called up again from below.

"I've reached ground level. You can come down now."

"Can you see anything?"

"Not yet. I'll start feeling my way around. See what I can find."

With the sounds of Matthew's shuffling footsteps coming up from below, Charles eased himself onto the staircase and began his descent. The first few steps were lit, just a little, by the light from the oil lamp in the room above. However, as he went lower, it became increasingly difficult to see and his progress slowed.

It was just as he reached the foot of the stairs, and felt himself step into the deep pile of a luxurious carpet, that he heard a triumphant exclamation.

"Aha!" said Matthew. "I think I've found a light switch, but does it work?"

He flicked it, and a wall-mounted fluorescent light flickered into life, casting a dim glow over the room, the two men – and something else.

They both stood there, not quite able to believe what they were seeing.

"Do you get that déjà vu feeling too?" Matthew asked.

Charles could only nod.

Against one wall, set up on a tripod, stood a screen. Facing it, from the opposite side of the room, was a projector, loaded with a reel of cine-film, all set up and ready to be viewed.

CHAPTER 10

"How long do you suppose this has been standing here?" asked an incredulous Matthew.

"I've no idea, but it must have been here for some considerable time. Clearly, the hidden trapdoor was deliberately made difficult to find."

"It looks pretty old. If we try to switch it on, do you think it will still work?"

"Only one way to find out." Charles walked over to the projector and reached towards the start switch. "Probably better if you turn the light off?" he suggested.

Matthew nodded.

As Charles set the projector running, Matthew flicked off the light. The enclosed surroundings and the carpeted floor gave the whole room an oddly cosy feeling. The two of them then stood there, in the virtual darkness, illumined by nothing other than the light coming from the projected image on the screen, and watched, transfixed.

As the film began, it almost felt as though they were going back in time. As on previous occasions, the film had been made in the octagonal room directly above them. There was the ornate desk, and several of the filing cabinets could be seen in the background.

After a few moments, the elderly Lord Alfred himself appeared, walking into the camera shot and taking his seat behind the desk. As he had been in his previous productions, he was once again immaculately attired in his deep blue velvet smoking jacket, even though throughout his life he never actually smoked. The handkerchief in his breast pocket was fluted perfectly, and it projected by just the right amount. Around his neck, a silk cravat had been tied, loosely, the folds of fabric suggesting an informal feel, while complementing the more formal cut of the jacket itself.

Once seated, the dapper nobleman looked straight into the camera and began to speak.

"Hello, whoever you are. I'm assuming that the fact you have found this piece of film means that you have already found my earlier letter and solved the puzzle in the poem, which led you down here. If that is the case, I'm delighted you have made it this far. However, I have to consider the possibility that perhaps you might merely have stumbled upon this room by some unfortunate accident; do not take offence, but I have no way of knowing for certain whether you are friend or foe, so I must still choose my words carefully. Assuming for the moment that I am addressing friends, I suspect that when you ventured down here you were expecting to find something a little more substantial than a screen and a projector. Am I right? Ha, I thought as much. Well, if it is indeed my letter that brought you here, then you will have already discovered how to make sense of it, and I am happy to tell you that I have employed a very similar device for the next stage of my puzzle."

As he heard those words, Matthew groaned.

"I knew it," he whispered.

It was almost as if the figure on the screen heard him.

'But don't despair. I promise you that this little conundrum is on nowhere near the scale of certain other trails I have laid in the past. It is simply that there are other people who will be — how shall I put it? — who will be interested to see what I have hidden away, and it is absolutely imperative that it be found only by those of whom I approve. Therefore, I have felt it necessary to include more than a single layer of security. I hope you understand. For a start, let me put this to you: have you reached the place which my original letter spoke of? If not, remember the falchion points the way. That alone should be enough to help you on your way but, since I am such a benevolent fellow, I have found another little piece of verse to assist you even more. I'll pause at the end of each line, in case you want to jot it down. Here goes."

"Do you have a pen and paper?" asked Matthew.

Charles shook his head.

"No, but it doesn't matter. We can replay the film later if we need to."

Bizarrely, on the film, Lord Alfred had hesitated. He was staring straight at his audience, with eyebrow raised, as though waiting for them to be quiet and give him their full attention. Now apparently satisfied, he began:

"Time is swift! Prepare to die.
Possibly may live forever.
Altogether, must be stoic.

Enter, then, the house and cherish
Trinkets, heirlooms — all most dear.
Every one so highly valued.

No one else, save thee and thou
Knoweth when to shout 'bravo!'
Only then will end the duel."

Lord Alfred stopped his recitation and looked into the camera again.

"So, there you have it. I hope you enjoyed my delivery. Once you have solved the puzzle and discovered my surprise I do implore you to take great care of it. We certainly wouldn't want it falling into the wrong hands, now would we? Thank you for your kind attention. I wish you well."

He rose from his seat behind the desk and walked out of range of the camera. The reel of film reached its end and the projector whirred to a stop. After a moment of groping about in the dark, Matthew again found the switch and the light came on again. For a moment, both he and Charles remained staring at the now silent screen, endeavouring to take in what they had just heard. Eventually, it was Charles who spoke first.

"I suggest we go and find some paper," he said, "and then come back and write down that new poem."

"Agreed, though I honestly don't think I can face another one of Dad's drawn out, protracted wild goose chases," Matthew replied.

"I know, but I don't think this is a wild goose chase, is it? We both know this is important, and we really do need to figure it all out as quickly as we can."

Matthew sighed and looked down.

"Yes," he said, "you're right. I'll tell you what – why don't you go upstairs and find some paper, while I stay down here and re-wind the film?"

"Good idea."

"But make sure you're not late for the second showing. There are no refunds. It's management policy."

"I'll keep that in mind."

Charles made his way towards the narrow spiral staircase

and began his careful ascent.

***

Something as apparently simple as locating a piece of paper turned out to be not quite as straightforward as Charles might have expected. To his surprise, the octagonal room did not appear to have a single blank sheet anywhere. So, having called down to Matthew that he would need to look elsewhere, he made his way back over the bridge and into the main part of the house once more.

The obvious thing, he decided, was to retrieve Lord Alfred's journal from the drawing room and use one of its blank pages to write down the poem from the film. After all, there may be yet further pieces of the puzzle still waiting to be uncovered, so to have all the relevant information in the one place seemed like a sensible idea.

As he hurried into the drawing room, his haste was such that at first he didn't notice Kristin, who was seated on the opposite side of the room in a high-backed chair, sipping tea from a china cup. He was pulled up short by the sound of her voice.

"What's all the rush, Charles?"

Startled, he swung round to face her.

"Kristin! You gave me a shock." Immediately feeling that he had spoken too harshly, he tried to affect a chuckle. "No, there's no rush. It's just that in a house this size, if you move too slowly you never get anywhere and never get anything done." He gave another laugh, but it sounded a nervous, and forced.

"Really? You didn't seem so busy before."

"Oh, with an estate like this there are always things that need doing, you know? By the way, how is your search for accommodation going?"

"Come and sit down."

"I'd like to, but, to be honest, you were right – I *am* in a little bit of a hurry."

"Charles, come and sit down."

Charles clenched his jaw and, with a momentary glance towards the drawer containing the beige journal, he moved towards one of the empty chairs and took a seat. Trying to avoid staring at Kristin's deformities was more difficult than he wanted it to be.

"James does make a nice cup of tea," she said, before taking another sip. She then set her cup down, deliberately taking her time over doing so.

"After hearing what you said to Matthew earlier," she said, "about the work being done in the walled garden, I was curious. Did you know I'm quite a keen amateur gardener myself?"

"No. No, I wasn't aware of that."

"Of course you weren't; you never asked."

"Kristin, I really am rather busy. Can we chat later?"

"So I took myself off for a little walk and, eventually, I found it, next to the maze, just as you said. What would you say is your assessment of how the work is progressing in there?"

"Well… I'm not really much of a horticulturalist. I leave all that to the groundsman. He's very good – I trust him completely."

"When was the last time you were there?"

"You know the answer to that. It was when I took Matthew there, to show him around and let him see everything that was being done."

"Charles, why are you lying to me? Nothing has been done in the walled garden, possibly for years. It's lying there derelict."

"This is starting to sound like an interrogation. Listen, I

am busy right now." Charles stood up. "You came here asking for some temporary accommodation while you got yourself sorted out. Out of the kindness of my heart I took you in, but if you're not happy please don't feel under any obligation to stay."

He walked purposefully towards the drawer where he had placed the journal, but Kristin's next words pulled him up short.

"I know about the poem, Charles." She had spoken softly, almost with a hint of menace. Charles slowly turned to face her once again. "Oh, don't worry," she continued. "The book is still in there, right in the place where you left it."

Charles was aware that he had begun to breathe deeply and audibly. His words came with an effort.

"After you walked out on me," he said, "once I was over the shock and I was able to think clearly again, I don't mind telling you that my respect for you plummeted. Now, all these years later, you suddenly re-appear, asking for my help. Thinking that perhaps you may have changed, I decide to give you the benefit of the doubt, but what happens? As soon as my back is turned you start prying into my personal affairs. What other drawers and cupboards have you explored? Do I now need to start keeping everything under lock and key in my own house?"

"Oh, darling, don't be so melodramatic. I happened to notice when you hid the journal away in there in the first place, and I just wondered what it was, that's all."

"All right, so now you know."

"Have you been able to discover what that strange poem means?"

"Not that it's any of your business but, no, I haven't." Charles was inwardly surprised at the ease with which this half-truth escaped his lips.

"And Matthew is helping you?"

Charles nodded.

"I'd like to help too."

"Would you, indeed? And why might that be?"

"Let me put it like this. If you did manage to find the little store of treasure that's mentioned in the journal, and if I were to be instrumental in helping you do so, might you be willing to put a little of it my way? That would certainly help me with my house hunting. We could part as friends, and I'd be out of your way before you knew it."

"And how do you propose to help? If you've read the poem, you'll know just how utterly cryptic it is. It could mean practically anything."

"Yes, but I like to think I'm quite good at solving logic problems, and the like," she said. "At the very least, having a fresh pair of eyes and ears on the subject can often open up new avenues of thought."

Charles considered.

"And what if I were to decline your offer of help?" he asked.

Kristin laughed. It was a playful giggle and, for just a moment, the sound transported Charles back to the time when the two of them had been so deeply in love – or so he had thought – when everything had seemed, somehow, simpler and more straightforward.

"Well, in that case," she said, in a mock serious tone, "I would just have to solve the mystery on my own, before leaping onto my horse and vanishing into the distance, keeping all the treasure for myself."

At this, Charles could not keep himself from smiling. Then he sighed, and sat down again, leaning forward in the chair and speaking earnestly.

"I will be frank with you," he said. "The money I inherited years ago has now all but dried up." As with his earlier statement, this one also was not quite true, but he persevered. "Right now there are bills which I struggle to pay, and –," he paused, not wanting to say what he knew was coming, though he did his best to disguise it, "… and I know that further substantial outlay will be heading my way soon. If I am unable to solve this mystery, or even if I *do* manage to solve it, but if the prize turns out to be quite small, I honestly don't know what I'll do."

Kristin considered, taking another sip of tea as she did so.

"Hmm. Well, despite all the surrounding uncertainty, may I suggest that our best option is to try and work together on this?" She paused, before adding, "Have no fear, I will do my very best not to get in your way."

As Kristin spoke, the smile she gave would have been quite sweet, had it not been for the deep scars crossing her face.

"My point is," said Charles, "even if you do help, there may not be anything for you at the end of it."

Kristin waved a dismissive hand.

"Understood," she said.

"Listen," said Charles, "Matthew is waiting for me, so I do need to go. Let me have a think about this and we can talk some more over dinner. OK?"

"Fine with me," Kristin replied. "In the meantime, I'll give the poem another onceover."

Charles crossed the room and removed the journal from the drawer.

"See you later," he said, before tucking the book under an arm and walking briskly from the room.

Alone again, Kristin picked up her tea once more and sipped, gazing into the middle distance, with a look of satisfaction etched on her countenance.

"Gotcha, Charles Seymour," she whispered. "Now I've gotcha!"

***

"Where have you been?" asked Matthew. "I've watched and re-wound that blasted film three times while you've been away."

"Sorry," said Charles, as he reached the foot of the spiral staircase. "Kristin wanted to have a word with me. Anyway, did you manage to discover anything new?"

Matthew shook his head.

"I think we really do need to see the new poem written down," he said.

Although Lord Alfred had obligingly paused at the end of each line, to allow time for writing, Charles still needed a further two viewings of the film before he was certain he had written it down correctly. Satisfied, at last, that the transcription had been carried out successfully, the two men stood shoulder to shoulder and read the words in silence.

"Well," said Charles, "as with the earlier poem, there is no obvious meaning, and just reading through the first and last letters of each line doesn't seem to help either."

"Quite, though on the film Dad did say that this poem used something similar to the first one. What could that mean?"

"I don't know – not yet – but let's not forget that other clue, the one not in the actual poem itself. Have we reached the place the letter spoke of? If not, the falchion points the way."

"But we have already followed the falchion clue," Matthew wailed. "That's what led us down here, so surely we must have reached the right place?"

"Or have we?" wondered Charles.

"Of course we have – haven't we?"

"The clue from the original poem said we had to look beneath the octagonal tower."

"Yes. So?"

"This is only the ground floor. We aren't yet beneath it."

Looking up at the spiral staircase, Matthew had to agree. There was no ceiling between the ground and first floor level, so the total height could be seen clearly.

"Yes, we have only descended the equivalent of two floors," he said.

"So I'm starting to wonder whether his clue about the falchion pointing the way actually has two meanings. That was a device he employed in the past. Do you remember?"

"OK, so if we're supposed to look beneath the tower, where's the way down?"

They looked around the semi-darkened room but there was no apparent exit, other than the staircase by which they had entered.

"We already looked around the outside of the base of the tower," said Charles, "but I suppose it's possible we may have missed something crucial. Perhaps we should have another look?"

"Let me see the new poem again," said Matthew. As he examined it he continued to speak, almost to himself. "What we needed to do with the first poem was to look at the first and last letter of each line," he said. "Then, in that piece of film, Dad said there was something similar in this second one – not the same, similar."

"Letters in the middle of the lines?" suggested Charles.

Suddenly, Matthew's face lit up.

"Eureka!" he yelled. "I've got it! Tell me, Charles, am I brilliant, or am I brilliant?"

Charles laughed.

"If you don't mind, I won't answer that until I've seen what you've found."

"Perhaps I should be sporting and give you one last chance to solve it yourself before I reveal the answer."

"I appreciate the thought," said Charles. "Please just tell me."

"It *is* the first and last letters of each line again," said Matthew, pointing at the page, "but this time they read from right to left, and it starts from the last line and goes upwards."

"So it's basically the same thing as before, but in reverse? Let me see."

Charles grabbed the book and looked at the poem. As he examined it, a broad grin spread across his face, while Matthew looked on.

"I do believe you're right," said Charles. "Once you see the answer, it seems so absurdly simple I can't believe we didn't see it straight away.

"Yes, but I can't tell you how delighted I am that I spotted it first."

Charles looked at the poem again:

Time is swift! Prepare to die.
Possibly may live forever.
Altogether, must be stoic.

Enter, then, the house and cherish
Trinkets, heirlooms — all most dear.
Every one so highly valued.

No one else, save thee and thou
Knoweth when to shout 'bravo!'
Only then will end the duel.

Sure enough, the first and last letters of each line, when read from bottom to top and right to left, spelled out a message:

Look under the carpet

Since the light in the room was quite dim, the carpet upon which Charles and Matthew were standing could not be seen clearly. However, they could feel, from the way their feet sunk into its deep pile, that it was of superior quality.

The room was large, and the carpet appeared to go all the way to the eight walls, gradually disappearing into the shadowy corners of the room as it did so.

"So are we just supposed to tear up this whole thing?" asked Matthew. "That would be quite a task."

"Let's look around first."

Matthew began to walk around in the centre of the room, scrutinising the carpet as best he could, while Charles began to explore the room's edges. The carpet had been expertly fitted, hugging virtually all the corners perfectly. However, upon reaching a certain corner, in a particularly dark area of the room, something caught his eye.

"I think I may have found something," he said, causing Matthew to come running over at once.

"What is it?" he asked.

"Look," said Charles. "This corner of the carpet doesn't appear to be quite as well fitted as the rest, and I don't think it's just because they ran out of tacks."

Crouching down, he took hold of the carpet's edge and began to lift. It offered no resistance, and it was immediately apparent that this part of the carpet was not fastened down at all. As it was raised, both Charles and Matthew gasped.

Despite the lack of light and the many shadows, they could see that set into the floor of the room was another trapdoor. It was rather larger than one would normally expect for a door like this. It was clearly very sturdy, and it had been reinforced with several wide metal bands.

However, the excitement which they felt at having made

this discovery was short lived, since there was no obvious way to open it.

"There doesn't appear to be any sort of handle," said Charles, "or any ring to pull, to help lift it. It must be locked on the inside."

Matthew leant forward and ran his fingers around the edges, but it was very well made, being flush to the floor surrounding it, so there was nowhere his fingers could gain any purchase. The only slight clue was an unusual narrow rectangular hole in the centre. It was about two inches long, but barely a quarter of an inch wide.

"What do you suppose that is?" asked Matthew.

"I'm not sure. Some sort of keyhole, perhaps?"

"If it is, it's unlike any keyhole I've ever seen."

"Oh, this is so frustrating," said Charles. "Yet surely we are on the right path. All the other clues so far have made complete sense. There must be some way to get this infernal door open."

"Perhaps we need to take another look at those poems?" Charles sighed.

"You may well be right," he said, "but let's do it someplace where we have better light. I suddenly find myself rather fed up with skulking around in the gloom. Better yet," he added, squinting at his watch, "let's talk about it over dinner. I wonder what Mrs Gillcarey will have rustled up for us this time?"

CHAPTER 11

With the discovery of the new trapdoor, Charles' earlier conversation with Kristin had slipped his mind, so as he and Matthew entered the dining room, he was momentarily surprised to see her sitting there – and all the more so, given that she had already begun to eat.

Having served her her meal, James was now standing politely and patiently at the end of the room. When he saw the two new arrivals he gave a nod of acknowledgement and busied himself with preparing portions for them too.

"Sorry for not waiting," said Kristin, as she continued to tuck into her plate of steaming succulence, "but I was starving, and I had no idea how long you were going to be."

"That's all right," said Charles, as he and Matthew took their seats. "Matthew, I forgot to mention, Kristin thinks she may be able to help us in our quest."

Matthew looked up in surprise.

"Really? In what way?"

"Since I was a child I've been an expert at solving logic problems," she said. "It would appear that the two of you are facing a whole slew of these at the moment, and they are not necessarily straightforward, so I'm guessing you could use all the help you can get."

"As a matter of fact," said Matthew, who was clearly irritated by the cockiness in Kristin's tone, "we aren't doing too badly at all."

"Yes," said Charles, trying to diffuse what he perceived to be some growing tension, "but, for all we know, there could be any number of further clues waiting for us, so I don't think it would do any harm to have an extra person along to help out."

Matthew didn't reply, but was obviously not happy with this development.

"In years gone by I used to enter competitions run by MENSA," said Kristin. "Quite often I would win, or at least be the runner-up, so I think I could be of real help to you. I promise that I won't get in your way."

"And what are you expecting in return for this help?"

Matthew's pointed question drew a sharp glance from Charles, but Kristin did not appear to be unsettled by it.

"Charles and I have already spoken about this," she said.

"Oh, have you indeed?" Matthew was clearly starting to become angry.

"Matthew," said Charles, holding up a hand in a placatory manner, "please do listen to what Kristin has to say. I think her help may well come in very handy."

"I assure you I am not a gold digger," Kristin said. " On the contrary, I'm most grateful for Charles agreeing that I could stay here in the first place, and my offer of help is my small way of thanking him. Once the puzzle has been solved, all I'm asking for is a small amount, just to help me get back on my feet, and I'll be on my way."

Matthew opened his mouth to speak, but Charles beat him to it.

"I think that sounds very reasonable. Don't you,

Matthew? In any case," he added, "let's not forget that we have no idea what awaits us at the end of this trail. It may be that there is very little to divide up, or perhaps even nothing at all."

As he spoke, though, both he and Matthew knew that this was an unlikely scenario.

There was silence then, as James placed generously plated meals in front of Charles and Matthew, and they began to eat.

Needless to say, what they saw before them was yet another culinary triumph.

In one sense, the meal was very simple; it was a traditional shepherd's pie. However, with someone such as Mrs Gillcarey at work in the kitchen it was never going to be just ordinary. The minced lamb was infused with a perfectly gauged balance of basil and rosemary, while the opaque sauce which held it together was an exquisite combination of tomato and paprika. The crowning layer of mashed potato was smooth, creamy and beautifully light, while the decorative topping of finely chopped leeks and melted mature cheddar cheese lifted the creation to an entirely new level. The rich onion gravy which was poured on top added yet another dimension to the overall taste sensation, while the whole ensemble was completed with the addition of a perfectly paired bottle of Rioja.

Having begun to eat before the others arrived, Kristin was now also the first to finish. She then sat, fidgeting, doing her best to try and disguise her feelings of impatience as she waited for Charles and Matthew to clean their plates. As soon they had both finally laid down their cutlery at last, Kristin could no longer contain herself, and began to speak.

"May I suggest that the first thing which needs to happen," she said, "is for you to let me see whatever clues you have so far discovered and to tell me about the progress you have made. I need to be brought up to speed."

Matthew shot another glance at Charles, who was aware of it but opted not to acknowledge it, choosing, instead, to respond to Kristin's request.

"Well," he said, "you've already seen the journal, with the letter and the original poem, –"

"Has she?" Matthew interrupted, incredulous. "Has anything else been going on without my knowledge?"

Charles ignored the barbed questions and continued.

"Since then, we have also discovered a piece of film which included a second poem."

"Did you say a piece of film?"

"Yes. It was always one of Lord Alfred's preferred ways of setting puzzles."

"Ain't that the truth?" Matthew murmured.

"This new poem led us to discover the location of a sealed trapdoor. We feel sure that the next stage of the quest requires us to get it open, but it seems to be locked from the inside. So far, we haven't been able to figure out how to open it."

"Can't you just break it open?"

"I thought of that," said Matthew, momentarily surfacing from his sulky mood, "but it's far too sturdy. You could smash that ruddy thing with a sledgehammer and it wouldn't budge."

"Could I see this new poem?"

"Sure," said Charles. "I copied it into the journal. It seemed like a good idea to keep everything together."

A short time later, the three adjourned to the drawing room, where James brought them coffee and petit fours. Normally, Mrs Gillcarey didn't bother with such luxuries; in her opinion they were too fiddly and time consuming to make. Not only that, but were she to go to all the trouble of making them, each one would be eaten in a single bite, thereby not lasting long enough to be fully appreciated. So, usually, it just wasn't worth the effort. For some reason, though, on this occasion she *had* made some, but her concern about the likelihood of them not being properly savoured proved to be quite justified. The three detectives had their minds set firmly on things other than homemade chocolates.

Charles passed the journal to Kristin, who all but snatched it from his hands and began to read the letter and both poems, avidly.

"What's a falchion?" she asked, after a minute.

"Turns out it's a type of sword," Charles replied. "There's one hanging on the wall in the octagonal room. It was positioned at an angle, so it pointed to the place on the floor where we would find the entrance to the lower level of the tower."

"I see, and that's where you found the film you mentioned, along with the sealed trapdoor?"

Charles nodded, and took another sip of coffee.

"It would be useful if I could see the film," Kristin said, "and could you also show me this trapdoor you've found?"

"I see no reason why not, but it's getting rather late now. Shall we reconvene in the morning?"

"Good idea," she said, brightly. "A fresh day and a fresh start."

As she spoke, she looked round at them both with a smile. Charles gave an acknowledging nod. Matthew, however, avoided making eye contact with her.

***

The next morning, after a hasty breakfast, Charles led Matthew and Kristin across the rickety bridge. Kristin struggled a little with maintaining her footing on the swaying structure, but she persevered and reached the other side without mishap.

Once they were all safely inside the octagonal room, Charles pointed to the falchion hanging on the wall, indicating the way to the lower level. From there the trio descended the spiral staircase to the carpeted room below. Despite her lurching gait, Kristin managed to cope with the narrow spiral staircase relatively easily.

A surprise awaited them.

The screen had fallen from its tripod and lay, unceremoniously, on the floor.

"How on earth did that happen?" Matthew exclaimed. "Everything was fine yesterday."

"I fear that is not the worst of it," said Charles.

"What do you mean?"

"Look."

He pointed to where the projector was standing.

The roll of cine-film had been removed.

"I don't believe this!" said Matthew. "Have James or Mrs Gillcarey been in here?"

"I doubt it," said Charles. "James can't manage to cross the bridge these days, and there would be no reason at all for Mrs Gillcarey to come down here."

"And look there," said Matthew, pointing. A number of heavy foot-shaped indentations could be seen in the deep pile of the carpet. "Someone has managed to gain access to the house, or at least this room, without our knowledge," he said, alarmed. "For all we know, they might still be here, hiding somewhere."

"Fortunately, I think that's unlikely," said Charles. "Look at this."

A line of the heavy footprints could be seen heading towards the wall and then seemed to disappear straight into it.

"There must be another secret door right here," said Charles. "Given the process of deduction we had to go through to find our way down here, I suspect that even Lord Alfred wasn't aware of it."

"Another concealed entrance?" said Matthew. "You've got to be joking." As he spoke he peered through the gloom at the apparently featureless wall. "Anyway, even if there was, how would they know about it in the first place, and how would they have found a key for it?"

Charles shrugged. "Goodness alone knows," he said, "but these footprints would seem to suggest they managed to do precisely that."

In the dim light, he began to run his hands over the wall and, after a few moments, was able to trace the outline he was looking for, at which point he gave a murmur of satisfaction.

"Full marks to the architect," he said. When we were looking around outside there was no evidence at all of a door on that side." He stood back and looked again. "Ingenious," he said. "Utterly ingenious."

Charles' feelings of admiration for the designer were abruptly curtailed as Matthew announced, "I suggest we get this door barricaded straight away."

"Yes. Good idea."

"It disturbs me to think that someone was in here while we were all sleeping," said Kristin. "Ought we to call the police?"

"In the circumstances," said Matthew, "I can assure you that the police would be of very little use. This is one crisis we are going to have to handle ourselves."

"In the meantime," said Charles, "I'll tell James what has happened and ask him to make sure that all doors and windows are securely locked for the whole house."

"Let's not forget the most important thing," said

Matthew. "Someone working for the Boss has taken the roll of film! Right now they'll be trying to crack the meaning of the second poem."

"What Boss are you talking about?" asked Kristin.

"That's a long story," said Charles. "I'll tell you later."

"But it means we are now in a race against time," said Matthew. "We have to solve this mystery before they do."

"How are we to do that?" Charles wailed. "We still don't know how to get the blasted trapdoor open."

"We can be fairly sure that they won't know how to do that either," said Matthew, "at least for now."

"So we still have a bit of breathing space," said Kristin. "Where is the trapdoor you mentioned?"

"It's just over here," said Charles.

He crossed the room and pulled back the carpet to reveal the formidable-looking reinforced hatchway.

"Any ideas?" he asked, as Kristin came and stood alongside him.

She looked at the defiantly closed door for a moment, appearing a little perplexed, but then her expression suddenly lit up.

"I think that perhaps I do," she announced.

"We're all ears," said Charles.

"I think," she said, "that we may need that sword from upstairs – the falchion. Could you perhaps go and fetch it for me? I can come downstairs without too much trouble but going up is a real nuisance for someone with my condition."

"Matthew… would you?" said Charles.

Matthew shrugged and bounded up the stairs quickly, returning a few moments later with the ancient weapon. With a flourish, he removed it from the scabbard and began to brandish it.

"*En garde!*" he shouted.

"All right, D'Artagnan, keep your hair on," said Charles.

"So what now?" asked Matthew, as he offered the sword to Kristin. "Are you going to prise the door open?"

"Hopefully nothing so crude," she replied, as she cautiously took it from him.

The blade was clearly very old, and flecks of rust could be seen at various points along its length. Nevertheless, at some point in the past it would have been a lethal implement.

Holding the ancient weapon carefully, Kristin held it vertically and then slowly began to insert it into the oblong slot in the locked trapdoor. After it had descended for a few moments, she felt it make contact with something inside. She then jiggled the blade slightly, before then giving it a sudden turn. There was the sound of metal scraping against metal. The door suddenly loosened and lifted a fraction, revealing a black cavity beneath.

"Quickly!" she called.

Matthew and Charles both dropped to their knees and pushed their fingers into the gap, trying to get a grip on the smooth surface. With an effort, and with muscles straining, they at last managed to raise the door to a fully vertical position, where it finally ceased its resistance and came to rest.

They now found themselves looking down at a flight of old stone steps, which quickly vanished into the darkness beneath.

"Wow," Matthew breathed. "Where do you suppose they lead?"

"Only one way to find out," Charles replied, "but we'll need to equip ourselves with torches." Then he turned to Kristin. "How did you know the sword was the key to opening the trapdoor?"

"I wasn't absolutely certain," she said, "but when I read Lord Alfred's clue about the falchion pointing the way, and when I then saw the slot in the door, I recalled something I'd learnt years ago in a school history lesson. A few hundred years ago, wealthy people sometimes felt that a lock with a regular key was not always secure enough to safeguard their most treasured possessions. A clever locksmith came up with a new design for a lock which could only be opened by using a particular sword. Since many people back then tended to keep their sword with them at all times, this was felt to offer greater security than relying on a key which could be more easily stolen and copied."

"Well," said Charles, "I'm glad you paid attention in school."

"You're welcome," she said.

"Right," said Matthew. "Where do we find the torches?"

***

It was only minutes later when the trio of explorers, now each holding a battery-powered torch, began to descend the darkened staircase. Matthew went first, followed by Kristin, and Charles brought up the rear. The stairs were uneven and narrow, so they moved slowly, and each step was taken tentatively, especially by Kristin. Emanating from their torches, the three circles of light, bobbing around on the stone floor and walls created a mysterious and almost uncanny atmosphere.

Before long they reached the foot of the stairs. They were immediately aware of a cooler temperature and, as they directed the beams from their torches, a damp-walled stone corridor was revealed, stretching ahead of them. However, the passageway soon bent round to the left, so they were unable to tell how long it was. Nevertheless, with determination they trudged along, following the numerous twists and turns which this underground thoroughfare presented, while trying their best to avoid droplets of cold water which occasionally fell from the arched ceiling and trickled down their necks.

At length, Matthew, who had moved slightly ahead of the others, paused.

"I think the passage is ending," he said, his voice sounding slightly muffled in the confined surroundings.

Edging forward, he stooped slightly, enabling himself to step through a low archway, while Kristin and Charles waited. There was the sound of a door being pushed open and, a moment later, they heard Matthew's voice.

"It's OK. Come on through."

"What can you see?" called Charles.

"You'd best come and take a look for yourselves."

Charles watched as Kristin squeezed through the small opening, before then following himself. As he emerged on the other side, he shone his torch around and gasped.

They were in a large, brick-walled room which was lined with many shelves, and the shelves were filled with large metal boxes.

"Have we found it?" breathed Matthew. "Is this the treasure Dad was talking about?"

"Let's see, shall we?" said Charles, as he stepped towards one of the boxes on the lowest shelf. "Hold my torch and shine it on the box."

Peering through the gloom, Charles examined the box. It was clearly rigid and well constructed. He tried to pull it towards him to lower it to the floor, but it was just too heavy.

"I'll have to open it here," he said.

The lid was a sliding one, held closed at one end with a large clasp. Charles became aware that his pulse had quickened. What were they about to discover? Gold bullion? Jewels?

While Matthew held the torch, directing its beam onto the box, Charles reached forward and carefully unfastened the clasp. Then, after exchanging an excited glance with his two companions, he began to slide the lid open.

CHAPTER 12

As soon as the prison officer had discreetly passed the envelope to him, the Boss left the exercise yard and his fellow inmates, and hurried back to his cell, where he immediately sat in his swivel chair and deliberately turned it so that his back was to the door. It was unlikely that any of the guards would spy on him at this time of day, but he wanted to take no chances.

Tearing the envelope open he pulled out two sheets of paper and unfolded them. One was a note, while the other appeared to be some sort of poem.

The note read:

Boss, we found a reel of film in a hidden room, though we're pretty sure Matthew and the others will already have seen it. It shows some old geezer who seems to be saying that the lines of a certain poem conceal the location of the treasure. We've looked at it but can't make sense of it, so we're sending it to you. What do you want us to do next? Standing by for your instructions.

Placing the note to one side, the Boss then looked at the

poem. He read it through twice, but it made no sense whatsoever to him and he swore, loudly. He glanced at the clock on his desk — another privilege from the governor. Yes, there were still a few minutes of the exercise period left, so he might just have enough time. Snatching up another sheet of paper, he quickly scribbled a message of his own.

Try to find out what the poem means, and I'll be doing the same. In the meantime, keep an eye on Matthew and the others from a safe distance, making sure you're not seen. They might lead you to what we're after, in which case we might not need the poem at all.

He folded the note, before placing it into the envelope and re-sealing it. Then he quickly left his cell and made his way back along the prison's numerous walkways and corridors to the quadrangle. He reached the yard and walked into the open air just as the bell sounded, instructing the inmates to return to their cells.

The Boss shouldered his way through the crowd of men who were shuffling their way back into the building, and headed towards the line of prison guards at the back. One of them waved his hand to indicate that he should go back, but another officer stepped forward and drew him aside. With their backs to the rest of the exercise yard, the Boss deftly slipped the envelope into the guard's pocket. There was a brief moment of eye contact, and an almost imperceptible nod, but not a word was spoken.

Then the Boss turned away and joined the rest of the prisoners as they made their way back inside the building once again.

***

As the torches were shone upon their new find and the

lid was drawn back, it was immediately apparent, and a little surprising, that both the walls and the lid of the box were unusually thick.

However, far more surprising was the contents themselves.

The box had been completely filled with high explosives.

"What on earth...?" said Charles.

Matthew was already sliding back the lid of one of the other boxes.

"This one is the same," he said.

"Wait a minute," said Kristin. "Where's the treasure?"

"I don't think we're going to find any," said Charles. "At least, not here."

"But all the clues definitely led down here," said Matthew.

"Yes, they did, but do you recall what Lord Alfred said in the letter? He said he had arranged a surprise, but he didn't say exactly what that surprise was. We all assumed he meant a stash of gold or something."

"So... are *all* these boxes filled with dynamite?" asked Kristin.

"I would say that's a fairly safe assumption," said Matthew. "How very like Dad to do something like this."

"How can you be so calm about this?" Kristin yelled. "If this room were to go up, it would probably blow the whole house sky high, and us with it."

"You're right," said Matthew, "and now I can see that was his plan all along. Look at that."

He pointed. From each box a length of thin wire emerged, which ran round the edge of the room towards a narrow archway on the far side of the chamber. At the point where they met, all the wires were twisted together and became a single cable which itself then disappeared through the arch and into the darkness of a passageway beyond.

"I suspect," said Matthew, "that if we follow that cable it

will lead us to a detonator."

Charles was incredulous.

"What are you saying?" he said.

"Towards the end of his life," said Matthew, "we know Dad made no secret of the fact that he felt like he'd done his innings and was ready to go."

"But if anything happened, or if any sort of mistake was made, all these explosives could have gone off at any time! Why would anyone put what amounts to a massive bomb under their own house?"

"It was a risk, yes, but he had clearly taken precautions. You can see that each box is very thick. In the unlikely event that any one of them did become unstable, I suspect that the box itself would have been enough to contain any potential explosion. As strange as it sounds, I think the whole thing was actually quite safe."

"In that case what was the point of setting all this up at all?"

"It's only a guess," said Matthew, sliding the lid closed again, "but I suspect his plan was this: if anyone unpleasant was to come calling, he would come down here and remove all the lids from the boxes. This would mean that the explosion from each one would be directed upwards. Then he would quickly run along to the detonator, and blow the house to pieces, with his unwelcome guests trapped inside."

"Would it have worked?"

Matthew looked round at the arsenal of explosives. There was a lot of dynamite there.

"See for yourself," he said. "Do *you* think it would've worked?"

"But surely he would never do that – not to Heston Grange. It was his home."

"Well, I wasn't around at the end, as you know," said Matthew, "but, by all accounts, as his death approached, he had become so jaded and fed up, I really don't think he cared anymore."

"What about James, and Mrs Gillcarey?"

"I don't know, but I'm sure he would have taken steps to ensure their safety."

"So… if the treasure isn't here, where is it?" asked Kristin.

Charles shook his head.

"I don't think there ever was any," he said, "and I already explained to you earlier that the fortune was almost used up."

Kristin looked as though she were about to speak again, but Matthew spoke first.

"As I see it," he said, "our main priority now is to decide on a course of action for when our secret visitors return, as they most assuredly will. Don't forget, they stole the reel of film and will now be aware of the poem. It's unlikely that they'll solve it, but I know the Boss, so I don't think they're going to leave it at that and just walk away."

"Who's the Boss?" Kristin asked.

"I'll explain later."

"Would it be a good idea for us to follow that cable, and see where it leads?" said Charles, motioning towards the wire which trailed away into the darkened passageway opposite.

"I was just about to suggest the very same thing," said Matthew.

Charles turned to Kristin. "Do you want to come along?" he asked.

"I don't think I will," she replied. "I think I've explored enough secret passageways for one day."

"I don't blame you," Charles said. "I'm sure James will be able to furnish you with some nice hot tea and some of Mrs Gillcarey's homemade cake."

"OK, I'll see you later."

***

However, Kristin did not go in search of tea and cake.

Instead, she made the lengthy walk along the drive to Heston Lodge. She moved quite slowly, and not without pain, but she persevered and was relieved when the quaint cottage finally came into view. At last, she stepped up to the door and rapped loudly upon it.

A few moments later, Meg's wrinkled face appeared in the door's glass panel and, after scrutinising the visitor for a moment, the light of recognition dawned and the sound of unlocking could be heard.

"How lovely to see you again!" Meg crowed, as she swung the door open. "Do come in."

As Kristin stepped past and into the tiny hallway, Meg stepped outside and looked around.

"Oh," she said, "isn't James with you?"

"Erm… no, not yet. I think he said he'll try to come along later."

"Oh, that's good. I do miss him, you know. Well, let's not stand outside in the cold. I'd best get the kettle on. Do go through and get comfortable."

Kristin was about to say that she was in a hurry and had no time for tea, but then thought better of it. Instead she took a seat on the small but deep sofa in the sitting room.

"Did James say how long he's going to be?" asked Meg as she came toddling through from the kitchen carrying the tray of tea things. "I need to know if I'll have enough time to start making some flapjacks – they're his favourite."

"I'm afraid he didn't give a specific time, Meg, but I'm sure he'll be along just as soon as he can."

"Oh, good. That's very good. I'm so looking forward to

seeing him."

"Meg, do you remember the last time I was here, you mentioned that Charles – Mr Seymour – had bought shares in a diamond mine?"

"Did I? I'm sure I may have done. People do buy all sorts of things these days, don't they? Not like when I was a girl. Back then, there were some days you were lucky to find anything in the shops at all."

"Yes. The thing is, to keep a house like Heston Grange going does cost a lot of money. Ever since Lord Alfred died, I know that Mr Seymour has been trying his best to hold everything together, but I think he may have lost track of some of his assets. From the time that you worked in the house, I was wondering whether you might be able to remember what some of them were. Then I could go and remind him – it would be such a weight off his mind to know that he had some other financial resources available."

"Well," said Meg, staring into space as she began to cast her mind back, "I'll try as hard as I can to remember, but naturally I was only a maid – just one of the servants. I wasn't really privy to His Lordships affairs."

"Of course, and I'm sure you were very discreet."

"I did my best. Lord Alfred was a very fine gentleman. I didn't want to let him down."

"On the many occasions when you entered his rooms, I'm sure you must have picked up little bits and pieces of information – information which would be very useful to Mr Seymour now."

"Well, of course, I did occasionally hear little snatches of things – but I wasn't eavesdropping. Let's be quite clear about that!"

"Of course you weren't. I understand. I know that you were a very professional and highly valued member of the staff. Can you tell me, though, where did Lord Alfred's money come from?"

"As far as I was aware," said Meg, "most of it was raised from another of his estates. It was up in Galloway, I think. I never went there myself, but I gather it was near to the sea a bit like here – and there were large herds of cattle and horses. Oh, I love horses! I would've so liked to have had the chance to see them."

"Did Lord Alfred ever mention that he might be selling off any parts of his estate?"

"I don't recall him ever mentioning anything like that, but I was just a maid so he wouldn't have told me even if he did."

"Thank you, Meg," said Kristin. "You have been most helpful."

***

The passageway was low and cramped and, as it turned out, rather long, but, with the help of their torches, Charles and Matthew were able to maintain sight of the cable and follow it as it wound its way through the underground thoroughfare. Although they tried their best to stay low, every so often they would scrape their heads against the rough ceiling above them and stifle a curse.

"When is this blasted passage going to end?" moaned Matthew. "I feel like we've been down here for ever."

"Agreed," said Charles, "but surely it can't be much longer now." Then, as he spoke, the light of his torch revealed that they were approaching another archway. "It looks like we're reaching the end of the passage," he said.

They squeezed themselves through the narrow arch and, a few moments later, found themselves standing in a small circular room whose walls were of brick, and whose floor was somewhat damp. As they shone their torches around, at first it seemed as though they had walked into a dead end. However, this was not quite the case. They were surprised to see that the cable which they had been following along the ground had here been attached to the wall and now rose upwards, gradually vanishing into the darkness above. Rising alongside the cable was an old, rusty metal ladder, bolted to the wall.

"I suspect we might be standing in a disused well," said Charles.

"Very possibly," said Matthew. "That archway we've just come through shows signs of being slightly more recent than the rest of the brickwork, so it's likely that it was added once the well wasn't being used anymore."

"I think you might be right, and it seems that the only way out is up," said Charles. "Not an especially attractive proposition."

"If we want to find out where the cable goes we have no choice. Shall we?"

"But how are we going to climb the ladder with our torches?" asked Charles.

"Hold it in your mouth," said Matthew, "or stuff it in a pocket. Didn't you learn anything from the Boy Scouts?"

"I must've been absent for that lesson."

With their light sources gripped between clenched teeth, they began their ascent, with Matthew leading the way. The rungs of the ladder were clearly old and decaying, and over the years some of the metal bolts holding the ladder against the wall had worked loose. Unable to speak, since their mouths were filled with torches, the two climbers scaled the wall tentatively. However, they were more than relieved to find that, despite the metal corrosion, the ladder did seem able to take their weight and they soon found themselves looking at a circular wooden panel directly above, which appeared to be blocking their progress. The cable continued to lead upwards, disappearing through a small hole at the edge of the panel.

They took the torches out of their mouths and transferred them to their pockets.

"If this *was* a well," said Matthew, "it looks like we've found its lid."

"Can you open it?" asked Charles.

With one hand still grasping the ladder, Matthew reached with his other hand and pushed against the wooden panel above him. It seemed to give a little, causing a plume of dust particles to rain down upon them. Charles began to cough and splutter but Matthew continued to push, and there was a sudden whooshing sound. Another large cloud of grit descended as the circular panel swung upwards.

"Can you see what's up there?" asked Charles, as he tried, without success, to fend off the descending shower of debris.

"Not yet. I'll have to climb in. Hey, maybe we'll find ourselves back in Meg's pyramid room again."

"Not funny."

Causing yet more dust to fall on the hapless Charles below him, Matthew scrambled up the last few rungs of the ladder and heaved himself over the edge into the blackness beyond. From his position in the well, Charles could hear the sound of Matthew's footsteps and see the light from his torch bobbing around. He called up to him.

"Well? Where are we? Can you still see the cable?"

"This is very interesting," came Matthew's voice from above. "You'll probably want to come up and see for yourself, but watch your step."

With an effort, Charles hauled himself up the remainder of the ladder and somehow managed to step safely from its rusty rungs, crossing onto a firm floor at last. Standing in the gloom he heaved a sigh of relief.

"I'm getting too old for this," he whispered to himself.

All at once, the darkness of the room they had now entered began to be partially dispelled as Matthew began to raise the blinds which were covering the windows.

It was immediately apparent that this was a one-room building, similar to a Summer house. The room was circular, and the windows ran round almost the entire circumference. Looking out, nothing could be seen in any direction, except for tall, thick hedges, and this curious small building seemed to be located in some sort of clearing.

A moment later, realisation dawned.

"We've surfaced in the middle of the maze," said Charles.

"And take a look at this," said Matthew. He crossed the room to where an old tarpaulin was covering something. "Ready?" he asked.

Charles nodded.

Matthew lifted the tarpaulin and moved it to one side. They had now found where the underground cable had been leading them, as they stood in silence, looking down at a detonator.

CHAPTER 13

The storm clouds had begun to gather again as Mrs Gillcarey bustled about in the kitchen garden, busying herself with finding the vegetables and herbs needed for that evening's meal. She glanced up at the darkening sky and muttered to herself, pulling her shawl about her, noticing that the breeze had suddenly become colder and more piercing.

Had the weather not been showing signs of another downpour, she would have taken herself off to one of the nearby wooded areas in the Heston grounds, to go foraging for her ingredients there. That was always her preference, and one of the reasons why she was able to create such tasty delicacies. However, today she would have to resort to recipes which were a little more basic.

"Mrs Gillcarey, you really should come in. You'll catch your death out there."

She glanced up as the voice of James hailed her from the open doorway.

"I'll be back inside as soon as I can, Mr James," she called. "I just need to pick a few more carrots, a sprig of rosemary, and some basil."

"Ah, I'm guessing that means there's lamb on the menu tonight?"

"Right you are, Mr James. Right you are."

A few minutes later found the two servants seated at the large kitchen table, with mugs of hot tea cupped between their hands. Mrs Gillcarey's wicker basket of freshly picked produce sat on the table, alongside a dozen jars of homemade jam, which were arranged in two rows.

"We're in for another bout of bad weather tonight, I reckon," said Mrs Gillcarey.

"I fear you may be right," James replied. "I think the only person who welcomes such news is the town's builder. He is probably already anticipating my telephone call in the morning, when I ask him to come yet again to replace however many of the roof tiles we are going to lose."

When the storms get really bad," said Mrs Gillcarey, "I can hear the waves from my room. The closer the storm, the more noise they make, pounding away against the cliffs. Sometimes, they sound so fierce I can barely sleep. It's a bit frightening, in a way."

"Your fears are well founded," said James, a little sadly. "Mr Seymour is only too aware of the erosion problem. I suspect he will be needing to look for alternative accommodations before too long."

"Do you really think it might come to that? And what would become of us?"

"Oh, don't you worry about that, Mrs Gillcarey. If it really does happen, I have every confidence Mr Seymour will ensure we are well taken care of."

"I suppose you're right. He is a kindly fellow. Anyway, I'd best get on and get that lamb in the oven. If I serve the master a raw dinner, perhaps he won't be so well disposed towards me after all. While it's roasting I thought I'd pop down the drive and see how Meg's getting on before it gets dark. I'll take her a jar of my new jam – unless you want to take it along for me?"

"Not this time," said James. "You know I always find it difficult to cope when her condition shows so little sign of improvement."

His eyes had become slightly glazed. Mrs Gillcarey reached out and patted James on the hand.

"Understood, Mr James," she said. "Don't you worry, I'll take the jam myself."

***

In itself, the detonator was not much to look at. It was just a plain, square wooden box, with a plunger and a handle. The plunger was currently in its safe downward position, with a safety catch holding it in place. If it were ever to be actually used, it would need to be lifted to a raised position to prime it, before then being pushed down again.

"The more I find out about Dad's clever little plans," said Matthew, "the more awestruck I become."

"What do you mean?" Charles asked.

"The location of this detonator, for one thing. By placing it here, in the centre of the maze, it's well hidden. The blinds were down, the door was locked and the thing was covered up. In the unlikely event that anyone did come into the centre of the maze they wouldn't be able to see what was in here. Not only that, but if it ever had become necessary for Dad to use this thing, the high hedges making up all those thick maze walls would have shielded him from the explosion itself."

Charles took a deep breath.

"So," he began, "now that we've found it, what do we do next? We thought we were hunting for gold or treasure, or something. Instead, all we've found is a room full of dynamite."

"We'll need to think very carefully. Whoever took the roll of cine-film will still be thinking that the clues lead to something valuable."

"Yes, but since it doesn't…?"

"They won't know that, will they? In any case, the Boss won't even be remotely concerned by all these clues and mysteries. What he *is* bothered about is obtaining what he wants from the Willoughby estate. Whatever methods may be employed to achieve that is not his concern."

"He sounds like a really nice chap."

"Quite. First, you received those typed intimidation messages. Then the roll of film went missing, so we know they've been inside the house."

"That's the most disturbing thing."

"I agree. In the short term, though, I don't think we are in any immediate danger, since they will be hoping we might somehow lead them to the treasure."

"The treasure which we now know doesn't exist."

"Yes. Nevertheless, we'll be OK for the time being. The longer they can be kept in the dark about that, the better. Sooner or later, though, we have to face the fact that his accomplices are going to make direct contact, and we'll need to have given some serious thought to what we will do when that happens."

***

That evening, as the fire once again blazed in the hearth, Charles, Matthew and Kristin sat in the dining room and savoured the mouth-watering roast lamb which Mrs Gillcarey had so expertly prepared. Infused with the fresh rosemary and basil from the garden, the meat was beautifully tender. It was accompanied by home-grown roast potatoes, cooked in lemon and garlic, with creamed spinach and a carrot soufflé on the side. The whole ensemble was bathed in a rich, comforting gravy, made with onions, shallots and a sprinkling of peppercorns.

James had ensured that a bottle of finest Barolo had been uncorked and allowed to breathe before decanting it. Then he moved around the table, slowly and with decorum, providing each diner with a generously charged glass, before giving a respectful inclination of the head and quietly departing.

It should have been a perfect evening.

However, each member of the group was taken up with their own thoughts, so there was virtually no conversation. Whenever anything *was* said, it was never more than something cursory and superficial.

It was just as the final mouthfuls were being taken and cutlery was being put down that James returned.

"I'm sorry to interrupt, sir," he began, "but it would appear that we have visitors. Two, to be precise."

Charles glanced at his watch. It was just after 7.30pm.

"Visitors? Now?"

"I did suggest that perhaps they should come back in the morning, but they were insistent, in a polite way."

Charles sighed.

"Who are they?"

"They didn't give their names, sir, though they were civil enough, and one of them is quite well dressed. As for the other, well... it's not for me to say, but they don't appear to be vagabonds or anything like that, so I've shown them into the library and asked them to wait there."

"Oh, very well. I suppose it won't do any harm for me to see what they want."

He was about to stand up, when James said, "Actually, sir, the gentlemen said they were here to see master

Matthew."

Matthew glanced up, his expression serious.

"In that case, I think I can guess why they're here," he said, standing up from his chair.

"I'll come with you," said Charles. "It might be dangerous."

"No. If I'm correct, for now they will just be wanting some sort of progress report. It's better if I see them alone."

"Well… if you're sure."

"Don't worry. I'll be right back."

Matthew and James left the room.

Charles, still seated and holding his wine, swirled the opaque liquid around in the cut crystal glass and gazed into the flames of the fire. He had all but forgotten that Kristin was still there, until she spoke.

"It was a pity that what we found earlier wasn't what we were all hoping for."

"Hmm?"

Still entranced by the flames, Charles did not at first realise he had been spoken to, but then it suddenly registered, and he looked up."

"Oh, I'm sorry. I was miles away. What did you say?"

"I was just saying that a room full of dynamite was not what we were hoping to find."

"No, indeed. That was somewhat disappointing."

"I had been thinking that if we had instead found the secret hoard of gold we were hoping for, I could have taken my little share and vanished off into the sunset, and would never have needed to bother you again."

Charles shrugged.

"I suppose now you'll have to revert to plan A and resume your property hunt again?" he said.

"Possibly, though I think I still have other options before I do that."

"You do?"

"Yes. You see, as it happens, I've been having quite a few conversations lately – with Meg."

"You've been down to the lodge? It's kind of you to visit her, but her dementia is continuing to deteriorate and it's becoming increasingly difficult to communicate with her."

"I've noticed that, yes, but it's also true that she still does have lucid moments. When she does, some of what she has to say has been quite illuminating."

Kristin's voice had taken on a hard edge. It was only slight, but it was nevertheless noticeable. With all his experience as a solicitor, Charles recognised it straight away, and he tensed, sensing that some sort of threat or ultimatum was about to be presented.

"You've been a naughty boy, Mr Seymour."

"I beg your pardon?"

"All this talk of the Willoughby fortune having virtually disappeared isn't quite true, is it?"

"I don't know what you mean, Kristin."

"Oh, you were never a very good liar, Charles. I think you know exactly what I mean."

"Even if I did, may I ask what business it is of yours?" Charles put his wine glass down. "You came here asking for some temporary accommodation, and I agreed. Are you now saying that you came here with other motives?"

"Let me come right to the point," said Kristin. "You are right when you say your immediate fortune has almost gone – that much is obvious from the general state of repair of this house." As she spoke she waved her arm, gesturing around the room. Then she paused and stared straight at Charles, fixing him with a piercing glare. Charles remained silent, returning the gaze without flinching.

Kristin suddenly laughed.

"So it's now become a competition," she sneered, "to see

who blinks first."

"You said you were going to come the point," said Charles. "You have yet to do so."

"Very well then," Kristin retorted, her voice suddenly filled with venom. "This crumbling old house isn't your only asset, is it?"

Charles did not respond.

"I must say," Kristin continued, "once Meg gets started there's no stopping her. She seemed to know pretty much everything about you. There's all your involvement with that diamond mine for a start, –"

"What do you want, Kristin?"

"Oh, and let's not forget the small matter of that large country estate up in Galloway."

"I said, what do you want?"

"And there was I, meekly believing everything you said about the fortune having all disappeared. So I decided instead to go along with your little wild goose chase, to search for the non-existent treasure in the basement, –"

"What do you want?" shouted Charles. He was now out of his chair, and leaning forward with both hands on the table, breathing deeply and clearly enraged.

"What do I want? I would've thought that was obvious."

"Years ago you could have stayed with me. I *wanted* you to stay with me. Then everything would have been yours anyway!"

"If you had treated me properly I wouldn't have felt the need to leave – and I wouldn't have ended up like this!" As she spoke, Kristin pointed to the ugly scars on her face.

"I did treat you properly," Charles whispered. "I loved you. You didn't have to leave."

"I'm not going to debate with you," she said, ignoring his comment. "You did not treat me as you should've done, and that's all there is to it, but I'm willing to let bygones be bygones. All I'm asking for is some appropriate settlement from you, so that I can obtain the care and treatment I need. You will then never see me again, I assure you."

"… until the next time you need money."

"Now, now, Charles, *darling,* don't be a sore loser. Just arrange a nice large transfer into my bank and I'll be on my way."

"Why should I? What if I refuse?"

Kristin sighed.

"Oh, Charlie, I was so hoping you wouldn't ask that."

There was an icy pause as Kristin and Charles stared at each other.

"You see, *dearest,*" said Kristin, "I have friends – friends who work for certain newspapers – who would be positively gagging to get a story like this."

"What are you talking about?" said Charles. "A story like what?"

"Can you imagine the headlines?" asked Kristin. "*Wealthy landowner spurns former lover!*"

"You're the one who did the spurning."

Or how about this? *Millions in the bank, but he won't help his disabled fiancé.*"

"I can't believe I'm hearing this."

"And just think what they'll say when they find out that a sweet little old lady who was a faithful servant for many years now has dementia, so has been turfed out and consigned to a tiny little hut of a building as far from the house as possible. Oh, it'll be sensational!"

"You're blackmailing me?"

"Oh, Charlie," said Kristin, pouting, "blackmail is such a vulgar word. Let's just say that I have needs which you can meet and, if you do, we can both then go our separate ways and live happily ever after. Don't you think that sounds a little more civilised?"

"I don't owe you anything. You won't get a penny."

"Ah, but I know you too well, Mr Seymour. You've always preferred the route of least resistance. I know that you don't have the temperament for a trial by media and, believe me, some of those journalists can be real rottweilers. Trust me, Charles. Just arrange the payment. It really is the easiest way."

Despite the hearty meal he had just consumed, Charles could feel his energy draining away. As Kristin looked on, he sank back down into his chair and stared into the fire once again.

***

When Matthew entered the library, at first there appeared to be no one there.

"Hello?" he called, a little anxiously.

No answer.

He began to make his way towards the far end of the room, walking quietly between the long, high shelves, all laden with books on every subject. When he was passing the poetry section, he had a momentary flashback as he recalled the many hours he and Charles had spent trying to make sense of the endless succession of clues in Lord Alfred's cryptic lines, all those years ago.

However, all thoughts of the past fled from his mind as he reached the end of the shelving, where there was a reading area containing two high-backed armchairs and a low mahogany coffee table. The chairs were facing away from him and towards the windows but, since it was now twilight, James had already drawn the curtains.

Glancing downwards, Matthew could see by the shadows that both chairs were occupied. From one of them, a voice came. It was deep and coarse, and it sounded anything but pleasant.

"Hello, Matthew."

Matthew gulped.

"Garret?"

"Hey, you remembered. I'm deeply touched."

He rose from the chair and turned to face him. The occupant of the second chair remained silent, seated and out of sight.

"The Boss wants to know whether you've got his money yet."

Garret was thin, with a gangly, spindly-looking body. He was wearing a suit but, although it appeared to be of quite good quality, it did not fit him properly. The fabric hung awkwardly, such that the end of a handgun could be seen protruding from his inside jacket pocket. Matthew looked him up and down.

"My compliments to your tailor," he said.

The man ignored his jibe.

"Where's the money?" he growled.

"I'm working on it."

"The Boss is losing patience."

"In that case why don't you do something useful, like exercising your brain and try to make sense of the roll of film you stole?"

Garret smirked.

"We were hoping you would be able to help with that."

"Like I said, I'm working on it."

"You'd better work faster." Reaching into a pocket, the man produced a slip of paper and handed it to Matthew. "This is my number. The Boss wants results."

"As soon as I learn anything, be assured you'll be the first to know."

"I hope so, for your sake. I usually prefer to work alone, but on this occasion the Boss asked me to bring along Mr

Jolly – only as an incentive, of course. It would be most disappointing if I had to allow him to actually make use of his extraordinary talents."

As he spoke there was a stirring from the other chair. Its occupant rose and slowly turned to face Matthew, whose Adam's apple bounced in his throat.

Mr Jolly was a mountain of a man. He was well over six feet tall, and he conveyed all the mood and patience of a coiled spring. Numerous piercings adorned his ears, nose and lips. He wore a tight leather waistcoat, from which his bare, heavily tattooed arms extended. His muscles were bulbous to the point that it seemed as though his very skin was straining to keep them contained. His hairless head glistened with pinpoints of sweat, and his jagged, irregular, broken teeth looked like a ruined acropolis.

"When we were trying to come up with a name for him," said Garret, "I suggested *Goliath*, but the Boss preferred something that would reflect his innate sense of humour. Isn't that right, Mr Jolly?"

As the monstrous creature fixed Matthew with a firm stare, its misshapen features twisted into something that might have been a smile. In the long silence which followed, Mr Jolly brandished a hefty-looking baseball bat, held in the vice-like grip of his enormous hands.

"We know you have things to do, so we'll leave you now," said Garret, "but please do your best to come up with some interesting news soon. Mr Jolly hasn't had much fun lately so I know he'd be only too happy if some suitable opportunity were to present itself. Don't worry, we'll see ourselves out."

Garret began to make his way down the long rows of library shelves towards the door. Mr Jolly, however, remained where he was, standing motionless, staring intently at Matthew, and looking him straight in the eye. Without warning, and with surprising agility for such a large man, he suddenly swung the baseball bat in a wide arc. Matthew flinched, but the swing was not aimed at him. Instead the bat smashed into the end of one of the rows of shelving. There was a loud cracking sound as a large chunk of wood came away from the end of the shelf, causing several books to fall to the floor in a shower of shards, splinters and crumpled pages.

Mr Jolly turned back to face Matthew again. Still cradling the bat, he gave a smile, of sorts, which was deformed and ugly. There was then the sound of someone ostentatiously clearing their throat. Glancing down the rows of shelving, Mr Jolly saw that Garret was waiting for him by the library door. Without a word, the hulk of a man began to follow, lumbering from the room and trailing the rough-hewn bat along the floor behind him. Matthew heard the sound as it scraped against the polished wooden surface, and tried to stifle an involuntary shudder.

CHAPTER 14

Sitting alone, Charles was still staring into the fire, and had become so deeply engrossed in his thoughts that he didn't register the sound of someone entering the room, until the person spoke.

"Where's Kristin? Has she gone to bed?"

Charles glanced up to see Matthew walking towards an empty chair by the hearth.

"Good gracious, I didn't hear her leave. I suppose she may have done; it is rather late."

"Well, I'm glad she's not here, because you and I need to talk," said Matthew, as he sat down.

"I guessed we might. What did your visitors want?"

"As I suspected, they just wanted to know whether we had made any progress with locating the treasure."

"Hmph. Well, we have, haven't we?"

Matthew seemed puzzled.

"What do you mean?" he asked.

"The progress we've made in our hunt for the treasure is the discovery that there isn't any. We misinterpreted the letter and jumped to a wrong conclusion."

"True, but they don't know that. As far as they're concerned, some immense fortune is still lying around somewhere waiting to be unearthed."

"They're going to be sorely disappointed."

"You're right, but they aren't going to go away. If you can't give them what they want by locating a secret stash, they'll expect you to come up with it some other way."

Not for the first time, Charles could feel his energy ebbing away. He put his head in his hands again.

"There's too much going on right now," he said. "I'm not sure I can handle it."

"I don't think you have any choice." Matthew spoke gently, yet there was an earnest edge to his tone.

"Matthew, I'm just a solicitor, an ordinary simple man. I'm not cut out for all this danger and blackmail."

"Blackmail? Who said anything about that?"

"Oh, no one. It's nothing. Everything's just starting to get on top of me, that's all, and I'm getting confused."

Illuminated by the flames from the fire, Matthew leaned forward, speaking with a mixture of seriousness and excitement.

"Listen," he said. "I never thought that my mis-spent past would actually come in useful for anything, but I've had an idea about how we might turn this whole situation around."

Slouched in his chair, Charles looked up, and sighed.

"Oh, Matthew," he said. "Frankly, I just don't think I have the strength for any more adventures and commotion right now."

"Fine. In that case, just listen."

As the flames continued to crackle, as the familiar sound of the whistling wind outside began to return, and as the darkness of the night grew deeper, Matthew began to outline his plan.

***

Kristin had slept, but restlessly. She had spent much of the night tossing and turning until the blankets had become mangled and knotted together, twisting around each other like some failed attempt at beginner's macramé.

She knew she had handled the evening's conversation with Charles well. The way he had lapsed into silence at the end proved that. However, although she had deftly managed to paint him into a corner with no apparent way out, she knew it was a foregone conclusion that he would try to find some alternative means to resolve the situation, before he would ever consider giving in to her demands.

That meant she needed a contingency plan.

So, when the sun had barely peeked above the horizon, casting a pinkish hue over the landscape and heralding the arrival of a new day, Kristin hobbled up to the door of Heston Lodge once again.

Before she even had a chance to knock, the door was opened.

"Hello!" called Meg. "I was watering the plants in my window box and saw you coming." She then looked past Kristen's shoulder. "Is James coming too?"

"Hopefully he'll be along soon," said Kristin, with an artificial, saccharin smile. "May I come in?"

"Yes, of course. I was just about to have breakfast. Would you like a piece of toast? I have some lovely homemade strawberry jam. Mrs Gillcarey brought it round for me yesterday. Of course, I would have preferred it if James had brought it, but it is kind of Mrs Gillcarey to do it, and it was nice to see her. She is such a dear. What was your name, again?"

"Kristin. My name is Kristin."

"Of course it is! You're so clever to remember it. Well,

do come through."

Once seated in the cosy, cluttered sitting room, Kristin declined the offer of toast. Instead, she had to wait, with thinly concealed impatience, while Meg nibbled away at hers, with maddening slowness. The toast, Kristin observed, was as black as pitch and burnt to a crisp, but Meg didn't seem to notice. She just kept on nibbling, whilst every now and then making contented grunting noises and occasionally remarking on how nice the jam was.

Barely had the final crumb disappeared between Meg's lips when Kristin leant forward and spoke eagerly.

"Meg, do you remember how helpful you were on previous occasions when I was here?"

"Was I? That's kind of you to say so. I like to help people whenever I can."

"Yes, you kindly told me about shares which Mr Seymour had in a diamond mine, and you also mentioned the estate in Galloway."

"Oh, Galloway. That was one of Lord Alfred's favourite places."

"Indeed it was. Well, thanks to your help we are now in the process of looking into both of those things, and Mr Seymour is so pleased. In the meantime, though, I was wondering whether you knew of anything else."

"What do you mean? I'm afraid I don't understand. Would you like some tea?"

"No!" A momentary pause. Then, with an effort, "No… thank you. What I mean is this: the diamond mine and the Galloway estate are both a long way away. Since you knew Lord Alfred so well, were you ever aware of any other assets, any valuable things, which he may have kept here, at Heston Grange?"

"That's a silly question. There were all sorts of things. This was his home. Of course he had things here."

"Yes, how foolish of me. In that case, might there have been anything secret?"

"Secret?"

"Perhaps some items that he kept hidden out of sight, due to their being so valuable?"

There was a silence then, as Meg regarded Kristin with a steely glare.

"Are you trying to trick me?" she asked. "I was a loyal servant of Lord Alfred Willoughby. Even if I did know any of his secrets I would never have divulged them to anyone."

"No, of course you wouldn't – but you're saying there was some sort of secret?"

"Not exactly."

Kristin could barely contain her excitement.

"What do you mean?" she whispered.

"I can't say. It wouldn't be right. I have no wish to besmirch Lord Alfred's good reputation."

"Meg," Kristin spoke softly, yet firmly, "Lord Alfred is no longer with us, but his successor, Mr Seymour, is in a very difficult situation and really needs your help."

Meg looked down at the floor and appeared somewhat sheepish.

"It was just a present," she said. "That's all it was, nothing more."

"Lord Alfred gave you something?"

"He told me never to speak of it, and I didn't. After all, it isn't appropriate for the Lord of the manor to give expensive gifts to individual servants. Just think what people would say!"

"What was it, Meg? What did Lord Alfred give you?"

Meg sighed.

"Ah well, I suppose it won't do any harm to say, now that the dear man is no longer with us." Then her tone hardened. "But you must give me your solemn word of honour that you will not go blabbing about this to anyone. Lord Alfred was a fine gentleman."

"I know he was, Meg, and I promise that whatever you tell me will go no further."

Meg leant back in her chair and stared into space, as she recalled the story from her rarely used memory. When she spoke, it was as though she was talking to herself.

"It was such a long, long time ago," she began. "Lord and Lady Willoughby had honoured me by asking me to go with them on holiday, to make sure their clothes were properly pressed, and so on. One day, Lady Willoughby was tired and wanted an afternoon nap, so His Lordship asked if I would accompany him instead. Well, what a privilege that was! I felt so proud. Me, a simple servant girl, going out with Lord Alfred Willoughby! Anyway, two lovely things happened during our afternoon excursion. The first one was that we came across a country fair, where one of the stalls helped you to make your own models – and we made a model sphinx. As a work of art, I don't suppose it was terribly good, but we both loved it. In fact, I think I probably still have it somewhere."

Meg lapsed into silence.

"Meg?" Kristin prompted. "You said there were two things that happened. Please tell me, what the other one was?"

"I've never spoken of this to anyone," she said. "Do you absolutely promise you won't breathe a word – not to another living soul?"

"Not one single word. Girl Guide's honour."

"You were in the Guides too? So was I. What a fine organisation it was. Very well, then." She adjusted her position in the chair and, now sitting up straight, continued. "As we were walking back to the hotel we passed a jeweller's. Lord Alfred said he wanted to buy something, so we went inside. Naturally, I assumed he was looking for something for his wife. Imagine how surprised I was when he purchased not one, but *two* expensive gold necklaces and handed them both to me! He said they were just a little thank you gift for all my work over the years, but then he added that he would appreciate it if I didn't mention it to anyone – and I didn't, not ever." She again cast her gaze to the floor as she added, "At least, not until now."

"How expensive were they?" asked Kristin.

"Very. They were both made from solid gold, and each one had a pendant studded with diamonds and rubies. My, what a lucky girl I was."

"And where are these necklaces now?" asked Kristin.

"That's the silly thing about all this," Meg replied. "Years ago, when I worked in the manor, my room was right up at the top of the house, under the eaves. Inside, the sloping ceilings made it look a bit like a pyramid. Well, the lower half of the walls was lined with oak panelling, and I knew that one of the panels was loose. The space behind became my secret hideaway! I had already hidden the other things in there and I was now able to add the necklaces and no one was any the wiser."

"Lord Alfred gave you other things, besides the necklaces?"

"Oh, yes. Like I said, he was a perfect gentleman – but it was all on the condition that I never mentioned it to anyone else at all. Not long after he had given me the necklaces, he also presented me with a pair of matching bracelets to go with them! The thing is – and I know this sounds a little silly – once I'd hidden everything, I all but forgot about them. After all, it's not very often that a simple servant girl would have the opportunity to wear things like that, so they rarely saw the light of day. When the time came for me to move out, I cleared everything from my room, but foolishly left the necklaces and everything else behind. To this day, I can't believe that I could be so forgetful – I'm usually so good at remembering things. Anyway, once I arrived at the lodge it eventually dawned on me what I'd done, but I felt I couldn't go back and ask for them, because that would cause people to ask questions, and Lord Alfred may have been embarrassed. So I just kept quiet. For all I know, the necklaces are probably still there, though it was a very long time ago, so maybe they have been discovered by now."

Meg then shifted her gaze and began to stare up at the ceiling, re-living distant memories, and a moment of silence ensued.

"I'll tell you what," said Kristin, after some swift thought, "when I get back to the house, I'll go and have a look for them. If they're still there, I'll come straight back and tell you. Can you describe which panel conceals the hiding place?"

"The room was only small, so there weren't many panels. If I remember correctly, the one with the space behind was in the wall opposite the door."

"And where exactly was your room located?" Kristin asked.

Meg obligingly began to deliver some directions, which Kristin did her best to commit to memory, all the while wondering how reliable these instructions would prove to be. Before long, though, the verbal map was complete and Meg sat back in her chair, looking suitably pleased with herself.

"Thank you, Meg," said Kristin, standing up. "I'll go and do a little search on your behalf straight away."

"That is most kind of you. It would be lovely to see my old necklaces again. Would you like a quick slice of toast before you go?"

"No. No, thank you."

***

Meanwhile, Charles and Matthew were nearing the end of their breakfast. Charles was quietly relieved that Kristin had so far not appeared this morning.

"So," said Matthew, "now that you've had a chance to sleep on it, what do you think of my plan? Do you have any questions about it?"

"To be perfectly honest with you," Charles replied, "I don't like it at all, not one bit, but in the circumstances I can see its merit."

"In that case, it's simply a case of making a decision as to when we put it into operation," said Matthew.

"Is there ever a good time to do something that you absolutely do not want to do?" Charles asked. "I just want this whole blasted business to be over and done with as quickly as possible."

"Are you saying you want us to go ahead with it straight away?"

Charles paused for a moment, then nodded, immediately wishing he had not done so.

"You're sure about this? Once we start, there's no going back."

Charles hesitated again for a moment, before whispering, "Let's just get the ruddy thing over with."

"In that case," said Matthew, as he fished in his pocket and pulled out the piece of paper which had been given to him by Garret, "I need to go and make a phone call. I'll tell them to come tomorrow."

Matthew's leaving the room coincided with James re-entering it.

"I trust that you enjoyed your breakfast, sir?" he said, eyeing the empty plates.

"As always," said Charles.

As he began to clear away, James then glanced at the third place, which had been set but not used.

"Will Miss Kristin be taking breakfast this morning?" he asked.

"I honestly don't know. I haven't seen her today, so far." He then abruptly changed the subject. "A thought occurred to me," he said.

"And what might that be, sir?"

"I was thinking that no one seems to have had a chance to visit Meg for a while."

"True, sir, we have all been quite busy, though I do like to go and see her whenever I can."

"Yes, I know, so I was thinking that perhaps I will give you and Mrs Gillcarey tomorrow afternoon off. Then you can both go and see her, and keep her company for a while. I know she'll be very pleased to see you, and perhaps Mrs Gillcarey could take along some of her delicious patisserie creations?"

"That is most thoughtful, sir," said James. "I will inform Mrs Gillcarey of your wishes."

***

In the study, Matthew was holding the phone receiver to his ear. His pulse quickened as he heard the call connect and the ringtone begin. He was startled when it was answered on the second ring. The voice on the other end was gruff.

"Hullo?"

"Garret?"

"We were wondering when we'd hear from you. You have some news for us?"

"Yes. Come tomorrow, at 2pm. We'll have everything ready for you by then."

"Sensible man. The Boss was starting to get jumpy. He

167

was wondering whether you were still a member of the team."

"Well, now you can tell him that everything is under control and right on course."

"I will."

The call disconnected, but Matthew continued to hold the receiver. Staring into space, he exhaled, deeply.

"Right then," he whispered. "Game on."

CHAPTER 15

The next morning, and after their recent post-dinner conversation, Kristin knew that Charles would not mind if he didn't see her for a while, and this gave her the freedom to move through the house, unhindered. That is to say, unhindered by anything other than her own physical limitations. The fact was that despite her recent therapy sessions, even the simple act of walking was becoming increasingly uncomfortable for her.

As she trudged along one of the many lengthy corridors of Heston Grange, she groaned as she approached the foot of a staircase which, in earlier times, she would have skipped up without a second thought. Now, though, she knew she would not be able to make the ascent without a great deal of effort.

Still, the prospect of what awaited her at the end of the search, together with the potential it would bring for improving her situation, spurred her on.

Soon, she whispered to herself, very soon I'll have what I came before and be out of this Hell-hole. I'll be waving Charles Seymour a fond farewell and he won't see me for dust.

Having thus encouraged herself, she grabbed the bannister, lifted a foot onto the first stair and, with plenty of grunting and an increasing amount of sweating, began the long process of heaving herself upwards.

***

"Not that I mind doing it, no, not at all," said Mrs Gillcarey, as she cradled a mug of steaming hot cocoa between her large, chubby hands. "Of course, if Mr Seymour wants us to go and visit Meg, then we must do what the master wants; and, yes, I do have some nice florentines I could take along for her, but I was there just a couple of days ago. She was grateful for the jar of jam, and we had a conversation of sorts – you know how she is, Mr James… meaning no offence…."

James nodded, and looked at his old friend across the kitchen table with a kindly smile.

"Of course, Mrs Gillcarey, I know exactly what you mean."

"… but having chatted for a while yesterday, I'm sure I've told her all the news. I'm not sure much more has happened since then that we could talk about. We might end up staring at the walls and not knowing what to say. I'd feel a little embarrassed, to tell you the truth."

As she spoke, Miss Gillcarey looked down into her chocolate drink. She hadn't removed the spoon, and now she began to stir, absently, leaving a thin trail in the froth as she did so.

"Anyway," she added, as an afterthought, if we *are* going to go I hope the weather improves. We'll likely be blown away walking down there if this wind doesn't ease up."

James glanced towards the window, momentarily

surprised. Inclement weather, and especially the seemingly unrelenting gales, were so commonplace in these parts that he seldom noticed them anymore.

"I have a suspicion," he said, "that there may be some other reason for Mr Seymour's request – something beyond his simply wanting us to keep Meg company."

Meg glanced up.

"That sounds rather mysterious. Whatever do you mean?" she asked.

"I'm sure I don't know," said James, with a sigh, "but if I'm right, I expect we'll find out soon enough."

***

The time was almost upon them.

Charles and Matthew sat together in the drawing room.

Neither spoke.

Outside, the wind had begun to pick up again, its characteristic whistling and whining becoming steadily louder as it resumed its exploration of every cranny and nook, and every rattling window frame throughout the old house.

Charles had his gaze fixed on the grandfather clock which stood against the panelled wall. It was just after 1.30pm. The deep, resonant tick of the clock had, for a while, been keeping time with his heartbeat. Now, though, as the time of the forthcoming ordeal approached, he had become aware that his pulse and quickened significantly. The stately, low-pitched ticking and the beating of his heart now combined to form a grotesque polyrhythm, and he realised he was being slowly engulfed in a cold sweat.

"Matthew?" he said, "I'm not sure I can go through with this."

Matthew glanced up at him.

"It's a little late to start thinking about contingency plans now," he replicd. "They'll be here in a few minutes."

"I know, but I'm only a solicitor. I've told you that already. My place is behind a desk. I've never had to even think about anything like this before, much less actually go through with it."

"I understand that. That's why I'm the one who's going to be doing most of the energetic running around. Your part in all this is far less active."

"Yes, I appreciate that, but –"

"Charles," said Matthew, cutting across his half-finished sentence and looking straight into his eyes, "you'll be fine. Stay calm, stick to the plan, and this will all be over before you know it."

"I hope you're right."

A thought suddenly struck him.

"What about Kristin?" he asked.

Matthew glanced up.

"What about her?" he replied. "I thought she was on the hunt for some new place to live, so won't she be out and about doing that?"

"Yes, I suppose so."

"Have you seen her today?"

"Well, no…."

"There you are then."

Charles sighed and looked back towards the clock, wishing that its relentless ticking would somehow slow down, and preferably stop altogether. Inwardly, he began to pray that something – *anything* – might happen which would prevent their plan from needing to go ahead at all.

However, oblivious of his feelings, the cold, thoughtless hands of the clock kept moving. Remorselessly, they continued their endless journey. As they did so, it seemed to Charles that the resonant ticking began to fill the room, becoming louder than ever.

***

In one of the lesser frequented areas of the house, part-way up yet another flight of unforgiving stairs, Kristin paused to catch her breath. Leaning heavily on the bannister, she reached down and tried to massage her dysfunctional legs, cursing under breath as she did so.

Then she looked up and groaned.

There were still many stairs left for her to ascend – and they were just the ones she could actually see. Up ahead, they vanished into the gloom as the staircase curved round to the left and disappeared from sight.

The sheer exertion was becoming too much, and for a moment she considered giving up. Indeed, part of her wanted to.

But the other part of her – the part which had eyes on the prize – proved stronger. She simply *had* to reach Meg's old room, right at the top of the house under the eaves. If what Meg had told her was correct, there she would find what she sought and, although her troubles would not exactly be over, they would certainly be substantially reduced.

Once this thought had lodged itself firmly in her mind, it gave her the fresh strength she needed, enabling her to resume her climb, with renewed determination.

***

"So the Lord of the Manor now has to answer the door himself. What a shame. Getting low on funds are we? Have you given the servants their marching orders?"

Regarding his unwelcome visitors across the threshold, Charles could not recall a time when he had ever felt so nervous, though he tried his best not to show it. Matthew had warned him about the appearance and general manner of the duo, and that of Mr Jolly in particular, but now that he was laying eyes on them for the first time he felt truly scared.

"No, no," he gabbled. "It's their day off. Quite convenient really, I suppose."

"Oh, I couldn't agree more."

Garret regarded his hapless host and smirked. The unpleasant face of the ever-affable Mr Jolly, standing closely behind him, also bore a cruel grin.

Charles couldn't help but notice his tattoos, which stood out, bright and vivid, while his much flaunted muscles appeared to be bulging and flexing threateningly. Worse yet was the evil-looking baseball bat in his vice-like grip, as well as the beads of perspiration which glistened atop his hairless head.

"Well, aren't you going to invite us in?"

"What? Oh, yes, of course. I'm sorry. Do come in."

Charles stood back and swung the door fully open.

"Thank you. It wouldn't be polite if we were to just come barging in, now would it?"

Garret stepped past Charles and into the cavernous entrance hall. The lumbering Mr Jolly followed. As he did so, he deliberately jostled Charles to one side with a hefty shove from one of his bulky shoulders. As he staggered back a couple of steps, Charles noticed that Mr Jolly had a long, ugly, serrated blade tucked into his belt. By anyone's reckoning, it was a nasty-looking weapon, and Charles felt as though his stomach had turned to water, but he managed to maintain his demeanour and, recovering his balance, he closed the front door.

Garret surveyed the surroundings, with the huge chandelier and the two sweeping staircases leading up to the balcony.

"Nice place you got here," he said.

"Erm… thank you."

"It must be worth quite a bit."

"Matthew is waiting for us in the tower. If you would be kind enough to follow me?"

"Oh, I'm sure Mr Jolly and I can be kind enough to do that. Contrary to popular opinion we are both quite civilised gentlemen really. Ain't that right, Mr Jolly?"

The mountain of muscular tonnage grunted by way of reply.

"Please, do lead on," said Garret, in a tone which managed to sound both civil and sinister simultaneously.

Charles began to escort the two undesirable characters through the house, along the corridors and up the stairs until, at length, they finally came to a halt by an open door and regarded the rickety bridge leading across to the octagonal tower.

"Is this some kind of joke?" asked Garret. "You expect us to go across that?"

"The room on the other side is where Lord Alfred kept all his legal documents," explained Charles. "Matthew is there waiting for us."

"Documents are not quite what we're here for," Garret growled.

"If I understand the situation correctly," said Charles, "your employer is looking for a transfer of funds. Isn't that right?"

"That was before. Now he wants more. That reel of cine-film was most enlightening."

"Did you think so? We couldn't make head nor tail of it."

"Don't play games. Matthew told me that everything was ready. That's why we're here."

"Hmm. I think it's possible you may have misunderstood

him."

In one swift movement, Garret stepped right up to Charles, invading his personal space and engulfing him in a lungful of bad breath as he spoke.

"Let me make myself very clear. There's obviously some sort of treasure or valuable item hidden away somewhere round here. All we need is for you to show it to us."

"Believe me, if I knew where and what it was I'd tell you, and you'd be welcome to take the blasted thing away – for the simple reason that I want rid of you. I'm fed up with all these uninvited visits and receiving threatening notes."

Charles was momentarily taken aback at his own forthrightness. Even the normally implacable Garret's eyebrows rose a little. Then he exchanged a glance with Mr Jolly, and chuckled.

"Oh, the mouse that roared," he said, with mock fear.

Mr Jolly sniggered.

"Anyway," Charles continued, reddening a little, "if there *are* any answers to be found they'll be in the room on the other side of that bridge. So are you coming?"

Without another word, he began to traverse the swaying structure.

The two thugs looked at the flimsy walkway. They looked at Charles as he crossed over and disappeared through the door on the other side. Then they looked at each other, and shrugged.

"Come on," said Garret, as he led the way with tentative steps, while Mr Jolly followed along behind, uttering obscenities under his breath every uncertain inch of the way.

***

As time went by, Kristin found that she was having to pause to rest more frequently, and for longer on each occasion. For the first time, she was truly starting to appreciate just how vast this ancient dwelling actually was.

Climbing steadily higher, the sound of the howling wind rose to a screech, as it whistled through rafters and around loose roof tiles.

However, after what seemed like an eternity, the misshapen remains of what had once been a beautiful woman reached their destination. Whatever state of atrophy Meg's brain may have reached, it turned out that the directions she had recited, leading to her old room, had been remembered perfectly.

Kristin's breathing was heavy, due to a mixture of exertion and excitement, and in the close confines of the narrow corridor it sounded very loud. As she slowly pushed the door open, ignoring the complaints from its squeaky hinges, she could scarcely contain herself as she caught her first glimpse of the sloping ceilings. The pyramid room was aptly named indeed.

Kristin flicked on the light and immediately observed, just as Meg had said, that the lower half of each wall was lined with wooded panelling. Wasting no time she hobbled across to the opposite side of the room and began to examine the woodwork. If one of these panels was concealing a hidden cavity it had certainly been very well designed. Still, the room was only small. Surely it wouldn't take a diligent hunter long to discover the object of the search.

Squatting down by the wainscoting, she began to run her fingertips around the panel edges.

***

Back in the octagonal room, the atmosphere was tense, and anything but cordial. Charles had never felt so uncomfortable in his entire life.

"This is just a guess," said Matthew, "but I suspect that the fact you responded to my invitation shows that you didn't discover anything useful in the cine-film you took. Am I correct?"

Mr Jolly remained impassive, while Garret sneered.

"What if we didn't?" he said. "So long as you give us what we're looking for there won't be any problem."

Seated at the ornate desk, Matthew leant back in his chair, placed his fingers under his chin and looked up at the two ruffians.

"Believe it or not," he said, "we really do want to assist you with this."

Garret displayed a moment of surprise but reassumed his icy expression just as quickly.

"You'll forgive me if I have trouble believing you," he snarled.

"Frankly, I don't care whether you believe me or not. It's the truth. See for yourselves." As he said this, he gestured towards Charles. The sorry figure was staring at the floor, noticeably trembling, and patches of moisture had appeared under his armpits.

"Yes," said Garret. "We can all see him. What's your point?"

"The point, gentlemen, is that our friend Mr Seymour is, by his own admission, not at all suited to situations like these. Given the choice, he will always choose the path of least resistance in order to regain, as quickly as possible, the quiet, peaceable lifestyle to which he is accustomed."

"What are you saying?"

Matthew paused before replying. When he did so, he spoke slowly and softly.

"We solved the riddle in the cine-film, Garret, and we've found a secret room."

"Where is it?"

"Not so fast. We need an assurance first."

"The Boss isn't in the habit of making deals."

"Oh, when you report back to him and explain what we've discovered, I'm sure you'll be able to talk him round "

"What 'assurance' did you have in mind?"

"The first thing to say is simply this: this house, as you probably noticed, has seen better days. It is in urgent need of very costly repairs and, despite what you might think, the money simply hasn't been there to do it."

"Life's tough, ain't it? Not our problem."

"Although the treasure would be sufficient to –"

"Ah, so there is some hidden treasure after all?"

Matthew ignored the question and continued.

"– would be sufficient to make a useful inroad into the necessary structural and restoration works, Mr Seymour is happy to forego all of that, and for you to take everything that we found in the treasure room, provided that you and your Boss then leave him alone to get on with the rest of his life in peace. In other words, he just wants you to go away, Garret, to go away and not come back. Do you think that would be something you could manage?"

"You're saying we can take everything?" Garret glanced across at Charles, who was now perspiring more profusely than ever. "He's just gonna hand it over and let us walk out with it?"

"That's basically the situation, yes."

"Before we strike any deals, we'll need to see what's on offer."

"I guessed you'd say that. If you'd care to follow me?"

Matthew stood up, crossed the room and pulled back a rug, revealing the trapdoor beneath. As he began to raise it he looked at Garret.

"Feeling excited?" he said.

"Wait a minute," said Garret. "What about him?" He

pointed at Charles as he spoke. "If we go down there, what's to stop him calling the cops?"

"He's coming with us, naturally," said Matthew. "I need him. Revealing the treasure is a two-man job, as you will see."

Garret considered, then nodded.

"OK, but you'd better not try any tricks. Mr Jolly hasn't had any fun for a while and I'd be more than happy to turn him loose on you two."

"Well, I'm sorry to disappoint him. There won't be any fun for him today either."

Matthew then disappeared down the spiral staircase into the gloom below. After a moment, he called up.

"Well, are you coming, or not?"

Garret glared at Charles.

"Just you make sure there's no funny business," he said.

Charles didn't speak. It was all he could do to shake his head.

Garrett sniggered.

"Come on," he said, and began his descent.

Brandishing the baseball bat, Mr Jolly glared at Charles and pointed to the trapdoor. Still shking like a leaf, and with the increasingly howling wind obscuring the sound of his footsteps, Charles began to descend the circular staircase, with Mr Jolly following along, uncomfortably close behind.

CHAPTER 16

"Are you ready, Mrs Gillcarey?"

Calling back along the corridor towards the kitchen, James was standing by the tradesmen's door, well insulated against the onslaught of the wind which they were about to endure.

"I'm coming, Mr James. Shan't be a moment."

Then, with much huffing and tutting, the figure of Mrs Gillcarey appeared, wrapped in a thick shawl, and carrying her wicker basket.

"Well," she blustered, "I've managed to pack a few things for Meg. There's some of my homemade scones and jam, and a few slices of Dundee cake, and I also made a cheese and onion flan. I hope she'll like all those."

"Mrs Gillcarey, you are truly magnificent," said James.

He was thanked for his kind words with a gentle push on the arm.

"Oh, you're such a flatterer," she said, blushing slightly, "though I do wish we didn't have to go out on a day like this. When it's blowing a gale it's bad enough, but later we'll be a right sorry-looking pair if the rain comes too."

"Ah, Mrs Gillcarey, you were never one to let a little rain put you off. After all, we are – neither of us – made of sugar."

"Right you are, Mr James, right you are. All right then, we'd best get on with it."

"And let's not forget," James added, "in truth, the lodge is not that far away."

"Oh?" Mrs Gillcarey raised an eyebrow.

"Well, not really."

"Hmm."

"Off we go then."

At the very instant that James opened the door, a huge gust of wind met them full in the face and, not far away, there was the sound of another monstrous wave being smashed into the soft chalk cliffs. Mrs Gillcarey squealed and grasped her shawl more tightly about her, as they stepped outside. With the gale increasing in ferocity, James somehow managed to wrestle the door closed behind them. Having first ensured it was securely locked, they then began their journey.

"I don't mind telling you, Mr James," Mrs Gillcarey wailed, trying to make herself heard above the surrounding din, "I don't like this. I really don't like this at all."

James did not reply, since the sheer force of the maelstrom and the howling of the wind carried her words away almost before they had left her lips.

Doing their best to ignore the worsening conditions, the pair of loyal servants trudged on, resolutely, towards their destination.

***

Grovelling about on her hands and knees, with pain and difficulty, Kristin was starting to question whether Meg's capacity for memory and recollection had been quite as sure as her manner had suggested.

The panel opposite the door — that is what the decaying derelict had quite clearly said – so that was where Kristin had begun her search.

Yet that panel, rather than concealing some sort of secret compartment, appeared to be the most firmly fixed and robust one of them all. Consequently, she had begun to look elsewhere, scrabbling about and carefully scrutinising every piece of panelling, running her fingers round every edge and pushing them into every little indentation, in the hope of identifying some clue which would lead her to what she sought.

But it was all in vain.

Although she hadn't yet quite admitted defeat, she did need a break. She slumped back against the wall and realised she had completely lost track of how long she had been searching. Now, gazing at the silent and unyielding row of wooden panels, she suddenly felt totally alone and a surge of utter misery rose within her. A single tear seeped from the corner of one eye and began to trickle its way down her disfigured cheek.

What was she doing here, she asked herself.

And, however much she felt she deserved some sort of compensation for all she had been through, had the whole notion of somehow extracting funds from her ex-fiancé been a stupid one after all?

As she sat there, contemplating her situation, the wind outside had become noticeably louder now. When the gusts were especially strong, draughts could be felt, as snatches of the turbulent air somehow managed to gain access through tiny gaps between the rafters, and particles of dust and cobwebs would be blown across the floor.

Back when Meg lived in this room, thought Kristin as she

surveyed the tiny space and its Spartan conditions, it must have been nothing short of sheer awfulness in the winter.

It was just when she reached the point of deciding that there was nothing to be found and that she should return to her room, that, from her seated position, something caught her eye and the faintest flicker of hope returned.

Could it be, she wondered – could it just *possibly* be – that when dear Meg had mentioned a wooden panel she had, in fact, been referring to a section of the skirting board instead? From where she sat, as she looked across the room it certainly did appear that one portion of it – the portion opposite the door – was standing ever so slightly proud of the sections on either side.

Not bothering to waste time standing up, yet moving as quickly as her physical infirmities would allow, Kristin dragged herself across the floor towards this irregularity in the woodwork.

Her observation was swiftly rewarded. As she drew closer it became increasingly obvious that this particular section of the skirting board did not quite appear to fit its space fully, and therefore did seem as though it might actually be removable.

With feelings of excitement returning, she reached out and pushed her fingers into the small spaces at each end. After a little jiggling and cajoling, Kristin gasped as she lifted the section of wood free, revealing a dark cavity behind.

***

Once the unlikely quartet had reached the foot of the spiral staircase, Matthew lost no time in making straight for the next trapdoor across the room in one of its dark recesses. No longer locked, he raised the metal cover and placed his foot on the top step.

"Hold on a minute," ordered Garret. "Where are you taking us?"

Matthew sighed and looked at him.

"I thought you wanted us to show you the secret room. If you've changed your mind, I would just as soon return to the drawing room and have afternoon tea. So, what's it to be?"

Garret fidgeted and looked uncertain, but his confidence returned when he glanced at Mr Jolly and saw the knife tucked into his belt.

"OK," he said. "Go ahead, but don't try any funny business."

Matthew rolled his eyes.

"You should watch fewer gangster movies," he said. "Come along, then. Oh, and you'll need one of these."

He picked up one of the torches which he had earlier positioned by the entrance and switched it on, before disappearing down the steps. After just a few seconds the only evidence that he was there at all was the light from the torch which bobbed this way and that in the darkness below.

"Are you coming or not?" he called.

***

Lying flat on the floor, and pushing her arm into the dark space behind the skirting board, Kristin groped about, her deformed face doing its best to display a look of ardent fervour.

At first, all she had to show for her efforts were handfuls of dirt and lifeless insects in various stages of decay, but then she gasped as her reaching fingers made contact with something that felt like a box of some sort. She could feel her pulse quicken as she sought to gain purchase on its smooth edges. Finally, she was able to achieve a firm hold and withdraw her find from its dark hiding place.

Indeed, it was a box — a moderately sized wooden one with a hinged lid — and, as she moved it from side to side, it was plain that there was something sliding around within. Ignoring the sounds of the deteriorating weather just beyond the roof, she sat back against the wall, and cradled the box in her lap. Gently sliding the catch to one side, she eased the lid open and gasped.

The necklace which lay before her was truly exquisite. The gold links, and the rubies which had been expertly set in place in the pendant, sparkled and gleamed just as brightly as the last time they had seen daylight, all those years ago. The sheer craftsmanship and quality were immediately apparent and, such was its beauty, the fact that there was only one necklace did not immediately register with the enthralled Kristin. However, it took only a few moments for this discrepancy to be noticed, at which point a puzzled frown crossed her brow.

That was when she noticed that the box was deeper than she had at first realised, and that it had been constructed like a sort of chocolate box, with more than a single level. With trembling fingers, she reached for and carefully lifted out the top tray, with its precious adornment. What awaited her on the level below was even more breathtaking. This time, the necklace was substantially larger. It had been fashioned with white gold, and sported five perfectly formed, multi-faceted diamonds.

Scarcely able to believe what she was seeing, Kristin proceeded to lift the internal tray once again. The third layer was home to the two matching bracelets which Meg had mentioned. Each was decorated with charms — made from smaller versions of the same stones used in the necklaces.

But that wasn't all.

It was clear that there was still one further level left to

uncover.

As she reverently removed the final tray, she almost fainted at what she saw.

The final compartment contained an astonishing array of precious stones, such as Kristin had never before seen. She thought she recognised some of them, such as the emerald and sapphire, opal and topaz, but she had no idea what the many others were.

How many were there? It was hard to say, but at a glance there appeared to be a couple of hundred, at least, and each one was expertly crafted and multi-faceted.

What would a hoard like this be worth, Kristin wondered.

She leant her head back against the wall and exhaled slowly.

If what Meg had told her was correct, and Kristin suspected that it was, then no one else on the face of the earth had any idea that this little stash existed. That meant she could take this wonderful box, with its wonderful contents, and calmly walk out of Heston Grange, and no one – best of all, not even Charles – would be any the wiser. Kristin allowed herself a small smile. At heart, she was not really a dishonest person, or so she liked to tell herself. Since Charles was unaware of this jewellery, it was not as though she was stealing it from him – not really. In a way, this realisation went some of the way to assuaging an irksome feeling of guilt which had been troubling her ever since she began to put her plan into operation.

But then a thought struck her.

Of course she wasn't stealing from Charles, since this valuable collection technically belonged to Meg!

Hmm, but with each passing day Meg was becoming steadily less and less aware of all manner of things, so it was only a matter of time before the existence of all this finery faded from her mind too. Anyway, perhaps Kristin could report back to her and explain that all she had been able to find was a single bracelet, and perhaps one of the stones of lesser value. Surely Meg would be happy with that?

Having thus attempted to pacify her conscience, Kristin gazed down at her newly acquired riches and considered.

After all her searching, and after all the difficulties she had faced in her life, was she now finally about to put her troubles behind her, once and for all?

***

"How much longer is this going to take?" called Garret in the darkness.

"Be patient," Matthew replied, from somewhere up ahead. "Almost there now."

Sure enough, moments later there was heard the sound of a squeaky old door being pushed open. This development caused Garret and Mr Jolly to increase their pace, while Charles was left to bring up the rear. Only a few further seconds elapsed before all four men stood in the gloomy surroundings of the room, which was piled high with dozens of closed boxes filling their many shelves.

Garret and Mr Jolly were amazed at the sheer number of these boxes.

"Is this it?" breathed Garret. "Is this the treasure?"

Matthew waved his hand.

"See for yourselves," he said.

The two thugs moved towards one of the boxes and began to slide open the lid. It took them a moment to register what they were seeing, but then their eyes widened in a mixture of surprise and fear.

"What the blazes is this?" said Garret.

With growing incredulousness on their faces, they quickly slid open another box, and then another.

While the two of them were momentarily distracted, Matthew and Charles exchanged a glance and nodded. Simultaneously, Charles darted back into the passageway through which they had entered, while Matthew sprinted towards the other door on the opposite side.

The sound of the two doors being slammed and locked shut caused Garret and Mr Jolly to spin round, alarmed.

"Hey!" Garret called out, "What's going on?"

He ran to the far door, but when he realised it was locked, began hammering his fist against it.

"Open this door!" he yelled. "Do you hear me? Open it! Right now!"

He looked at Mr Jolly and nodded towards the other door. The lumbering fellow lurched towards it but had just as little success in securing their exit there.

They were trapped.

***

Meanwhile, as arranged, Charles was racing back along the passageway towards the octagonal tower as fast as he could, with his fingers firmly crossed and adrenalin coursing through him. The plan was in motion and he knew there could be no turning back now.

At the same moment, Matthew was haring in the opposite direction along the other underground thoroughfare. Upon reaching the end, where the old, rusty ladder awaited him, he climbed rapidly upwards, ascending the rungs two at a time, and finally swinging himself through the trapdoor at the top.

***

"Smash it in!" screamed Garret. "Break the ruddy thing

down!"

Mr Jolly hefted the baseball bat and began to direct one swing after another at the locked door.

***

Now some distance away, Charles had almost reached the tower when the sounds of the escape attempt reached him. In the confines of the narrow passage, the heavy blows on the door sounded thunderous. He had no way of knowing whether the door would withstand the onslaught, and a surge of fear gave him fresh energy. He further increased his pace and, for the first time in decades, whispered a prayer under his breath.

***

Once Matthew had climbed up through the floor into the hut in the centre of the maze, he raced across to the large tarpaulin. Taking hold of it, he threw it aside, revealing the detonator beneath.

***

The solid oak door was doing its best to thwart the attempts of Mr Jolly to break through it, but this ogre of a man was not easily dissuaded. As the assault continued, cracks were beginning to appear, as shards and fragments of oak splintered off in all directions.

"Hurry up!" screamed Garret, glancing again nervously at the numerous boxes filling the room.

***

Having made a swift check to ensure that the fuse wire was still attached, Matthew flicked open the safety catch, then grabbed the detonator's plunger and pulled it up. The device was now primed and ready.

***

Carrying her newly acquired box of treasures and, with it, the promise of distinct and significant improvement in the quality of her life, Kristin emerged from the pyramid room and began to negotiate the first of the numerous staircases and lengthy corridors she would need to navigate on the way back to her room. From there, she decided, she would simply pack her things and leave. There was no longer any love lost between her and Charles, so the saying of farewells was a pointless exercise and a waste of valuable time.

Best to just quietly slip away.

Anyway, she told herself, Charles was so taken up with all those pointless poems and all that treasure nonsense, he probably wouldn't even notice she'd gone.

***

Charles had now reached the lower level of the octagonal tower and, as swiftly as he could, was climbing the spiral staircase towards Lord Alfred's office.

"Hurry," he whispered under his breath. "Faster. Faster."

He reached the upper level and made straight for the main house once again. He was halfway back across the rickety bridge when an uninvited thought suddenly struck him.

Where was Kristin?

***

The repeated blows from Mr Jolly were finally starting to make some headway. It was clear that the aged door was now starting to weaken.

"When we get out of here, we'll teach those buggers a lesson they won't forget in a hurry," Garret snarled.

Mr Jolly paused in his onslaught just long enough to flash Garret an evil grin before he returned to the task in hand with renewed effort.

***

In the hut in the centre of the maze, Matthew crouched, with both hands firmly holding the plunger. Although the sounds of Mr Jolly's aggressive attack on the closed door could be heard faintly in the distance, Matthew was oblivious to them. Other than the sound of his deep breathing, there was a palpable stillness within the hut itself.

Yet, despite all the planning and all the discussions with Charles, now that the moment had finally come, Matthew found himself hesitating.

Was he really going to do this?

Well, of course he was.

He had to.

And yet....

And yet....

Did he actually have it within him to do it?

Really?

Heston Grange held unhappy memories for him – that much was certainly true – but it had also been his home.

He looked down again at the detonator. All it would take was one push. That was all. Just one moment of courage, and it would be done.

Just one push....

***

Yet another relentless bombardment of blows and the door was now all but hanging off its hinges, with the passageway beyond now steadily coming into view.

"Good work, Mr Jolly," Garret growled. His face was a mask of fury, as the final fragments of the door began to fall away.

***

The sound of Mr Jolly's onslaught carrying along the passageway finally managed to permeate its way into Matthew's conscious thoughts.

He knew the moment had come.

His palms were sweating as he tightened his grip on the plunger.

"Now or never," he breathed. "So long, Heston Grange. It's been fun."

He took a final deep breath and then, with a scream of determination, he pushed the handle down.

CHAPTER 17

For what felt like one long moment, nothing seemed to happen.

Once the plunger had been thrust down, there was just enough time for Matthew to start wondering whether the fuse wire had somehow become severed somewhere in the passageway, and that the plan wasn't going to work after all, when –

Despite his being a safe distance away, the sheer volume and power of the explosion was terrifying. Even having braced himself against the blast, Matthew, with his hands still on the plunger, felt his spine jarring at the force of it and he felt his head swim. The walls of the hut shook and its windows rattled, and clouds of dust and cobwebs fell from the beams above, filling the air with clouds of dirt and grit.

He staggered to the door, threw it open, and lurched outside. Having discovered the previous day that the way through the maze was not especially difficult to remember, he gave himself a mental pat on the back for his forethought. Then, as his head gradually continued to clear from the force of the blast, he hastened along the many high-hedged pathways, whose tops were being blown back and forth by the ferocious wind, which continued unabated.

***

Kristin was part-way down yet another staircase when she heard the explosion. The steps beneath her feet shifted and she momentarily lost her balance, grabbing the bannister with one hand to steady herself, while carefully holding her box of treasures in the other.

What on earth was that, she wondered. Whatever it was, it sounded as though it had come from several floors below, and it was clearly something very serious.

She paused, and listened. Although she heard nothing further, she did her best to increase her pace. Now all she wanted was to just get out of there as quickly as possible.

***

With their heads bent into the increasingly strong wind, James and Mrs Gillcarey had almost reached the lodge when the explosion occurred, and it stopped them in their tracks.

They span round to look, but the house itself was hidden from view by the many trees in the grounds. Mrs Gillcarey grabbed James' elbow.

"Oh, my dear Lord," she whispered, "whatever has happened?"

"I'm sure I don't know," James replied, "but I should go and find out. Mrs Gillcarey, please make your way to the Lodge. From there, call the fire brigade and make sure Meg is all right. Then wait for me. I must return to the house immediately."

"Right you are, Mr James," she replied, "but do take care of yourself. Please do."

***

Once the lids had been removed, the clever design of the boxes holding the dynamite had caused the blast to be directed straight upwards. The force had ripped straight through the floor of the entrance hall, leaving a great many splintered and fractured floorboards and a large, gaping hole. The wooden pillar in the centre, which held up the two sweeping staircases, teetered uncertainly on the brink of the newly formed chasm. For a moment, it seemed as though it might be able to maintain its position, but then gravity took its toll and it went toppling into the abyss. As it did so, the staircase on the left, now without its support, also collapsed. Joints and nails screeched as they reluctantly came away, and the one remaining staircase, with the balcony above, wobbled and began to sway.

The sound of all that creaking, scraping and snapping was truly hideous. Around the foyer, paintings, which had hung on the walls for years, were dislodged and went crashing down to what remained of the floor, while a solid metal lampstand fell sideways against a bureau before rolling off and dropping through the hole.

There was also another effect of the explosion, something which neither Charles nor Matthew had anticipated.

In a seldom explored cupboard below stairs was the electric fuse box, where much of the wiring was very old. The task of attending to the re-wiring had been on Charles' list of things to be done, but he hadn't yet got around to it.

When the huge blast in the cellar occurred, its force caused the wiring attachments, already loosened with age, to come adrift completely. Bare neutral and live wires suddenly came into contact.

There was a spark.

Then another.

And then a flame.

***

The largest of the cars – an elegant limousine with plenty of space for both passengers and luggage – had been loaded the night before with essential supplies and all important pieces of documentation. The plan had been that, after the explosion, Charles would get out of the house as rapidly as he could, then drive firstly to the maze, where he would collect Matthew, before progressing to the Lodge, where James, Meg and Mrs Gillcarey would join them.

Now, though, instead of heading for the car, Charles was racing down the long corridors in the direction of Kristin's room. He was aware of a quiet thought somewhere in the back of his mind trying to tell him it was most unlikely she would be there – surely she would have heard the explosion and made her own way out of the house? Yet, he couldn't be certain, so felt he had an obligation to at least try to warn her.

At last, he reached her room and flung the door open. On the bed was an open suitcase, bearing the appearance of having been partially packed, but of Kristin herself there was no sign.

He tried to fight the urge to panic. Surely she was OK. Surely she must have left the building and reached safety. Hadn't she?

"Kristin!" he shouted down the empty passageway, looking left and right. "Kristin!"

There was no reply.

Then he saw the flames.

At the far end of the corridor, the wooden panelling was being quickly eaten up by the voracious tongues of fire. Charles ran a few steps towards it, but immediately realised that the blaze had already taken hold and there was nothing he could do to stop it.

Frantically, he ran in the opposite direction and darted into one of the side rooms where he snatched up a telephone and dialled 999.

"Hello?" he yelled, pushing the button on top of the phone. "Hello? Can anyone hear me?"

The line was dead.

Charles swore and raced back out into the corridor. The flames were closer now, and clouds of black smoke were starting to fill the corridor.

"Kristin!" he shouted again, as he began to run, but there was still no reply.

It was no use.

He had to get out – and fast – and he just had to hope that Kristin had somehow managed to escape too.

He clamped a hand over his mouth in a vain attempt to keep the increasingly acrid smoke from his lungs, as he raced down the long passageways, trying to outrun the flames which were pursuing him.

***

Matthew finally emerged from the maze and stopped in his tracks at the sight which awaited him.

Heston Grange, a once proud and magnificent dwelling, had become an inferno. Although the stone structural elements of the house still stood, it was clear that much of the wooden interior was ablaze. The powerful winds fanned the flames, inciting them to greater fury and causing them to reach high into the sky, as their deep yellows and reds gorged themselves on their new-found fuel.

Matthew stood there, open-mouthed and aghast.

"What have I done?" he whispered.

"I beg your pardon, sir?"

Obscured by the sound of the wind, Matthew had not heard James approach and was startled to see the elderly servant at his side.

"Oh, James," he gabbled, "I can't believe what I'm seeing."

"Has the fire brigade been called?" James asked.

"I... I don't know. I assume Charles will have done that." Then he looked around, suddenly alarmed.

"Charles! Where is he? James, have you seen him?"

James shook his head.

"Wait here," Matthew yelled, and began to run towards the house.

"Do take care, sir," James called after him, though the wind carried his voice away and the departing Matthew didn't hear it.

With his head bent against the wind, James continued to watch, with a tear in his eye, as the flames continued to increase in ferocity. A little further away, just beyond the house, he could also see ocean spray being flung into the air, as the waves of the ocean were whipped into a frenzy by the wild winds, and were slammed again and again into the soft chalk cliffs.

***

Breathlessly, Charles came running into the entrance hall and skidded to a halt, just in time to prevent himself from falling headlong into the huge gaping hole in the floor, which now blocked his way and prevented him from taking his intended route to the waiting car outside.

Although the sound of the roaring fire could be heard, it had not yet reached this part of the house, but the devastation already wrought by the blast was severe. The broken and jagged strips of wood, torn from floor, walls, pillars and stairs were strewn everywhere. Some paintings still clung, stoically, to the wall, hanging lopsided and holding on by one corner, while others had been ripped from their smashed frames, and ornate chairs were now balanced precariously on the edge of the recently created chasm, looking as though they might topple in at any moment.

Charles forced himself to stop and think calmly. From here, how could he best reach the car so he could go and collect everyone else, as planned? Momentarily lost in his thoughts, with the wind howling and raging outside, and with the sound of the approaching flames, Charles almost didn't hear the voice calling his name.

"Charles! Charles!"

The entrance hall was now starting to fill with smoke. It created a disorienting effect and Charles couldn't be sure which direction the voice was coming from.

"Charles! Help me! Please! Charles!"

And then he saw, on the balcony which overlooked the entrance hall at first floor level, Kristin standing there at what had been the top of the now collapsed staircase. She appeared to be holding some sort of box and was obviously distressed. Tears had left silvery trails down her cheeks, and her face was speckled with soot.

"How do I get down?" she wailed.

"Use the other stairs!" called Charles, pointing to the flight on the other side of the hall.

He watched, anxiously, as Kristin nodded and began to lurch her way towards it.

After reaching the top, it was just as she put her foot on the first step that Charles spotted the supporting pillars beneath, which were now bowed and cracking. One of them suddenly fell away completely, causing the staircase to sag, and lurch precariously to one side, though Kristin didn't seem to notice and continued her descent.

"Stop!" Charles called up to her. "Wait! It's too dangerous!"

"What? What did you say?" called Kristin, above the increasing noise as she set her foot on the second step.

"Don't use the stairs!" he screamed. "We'll have to figure out another way to get you down."

Kristin glanced again at the flames, which were now very close indeed, and the intensity of their heat could be felt. "There's no time," she called back. "I'll have to risk it."

Charles swiftly assessed the situation, and her chances of reaching ground level safely.

"If you walk very close to the wall the stairs might still be able to take your weight," he yelled up at her, "but leave that box behind – you'll need both hands to steady yourself."

Charles wasn't sure whether or not she had heard him, but Kristin did not put the box down. Instead, she held it close to her chest with one hand, while using the other to steady herself against the wall. Then, tentatively, she resumed her descent, taking first one step, then another, but progress was slow and the fire was not showing any sign of abating.

Charles kept looking back and forth, first at the approaching flames and then back at Kristin. Would she be able to get down in time? The situation did not look promising. Suddenly, there was an ear-splitting crack as the last remaining pillar supporting the staircase gave way. Kristin howled as the steps vanished from beneath her. As she fell, by some miracle her one free hand desperately reached out and managed to grab what little remained of the bannister. Shrieking, she was now left suspended, hanging there and swinging to and fro, while holding on to the rail with one hand, and somehow still clutching the box with the other.

"Charles, help me!" she screamed.

From his vantage point, Charles could see that despite her perilous situation, the very edges of the stairs still protruded from the wall. It was just possible, he surmised, that Kristin could make her descent by clinging to the wall and using the remains of the steps as footholds.

"Kristin!" he called up to her. "I think I can see a way down. You can make use of those narrow ends of each stair, but you'll need both hands free. You're going to have to leave that box behind."

"No," she yelled back. "I can make it. I can still make it."

Helpless, Charles watched anxiously as Kristin began to edge her way down this very narrowest of staircases. She managed to take one step down, and then another. Then, as she brought her weight to bear on the third step, the already weakened wood suddenly gave out.

The broken fragments fell to the floor below, and Kristin screamed and lost her balance. She made a desperate grab at the handrail once again, but the fingers of her one free hand grasped only thin air.

Charles could do nothing but stand and stare as Kristin's body, with arms and legs flailing, fell from where the stairs had been. The box she had been so desperate to hold on to slipped from her hand. Charles gasped as the lid sprang open and a cascade of jewellery and precious stones went tumbling into the abyss.

"Chaaaaaaarles!" she shrieked, as she fell straight past him and plunged through the jagged hole in the floor. A moment later, there was a sickening crunch and her scream was abruptly silenced.

CHAPTER 18

"No!" cried Charles. The mixture of feelings and emotions which welled up within caused a wave of nausea to surge through him. He staggered to one side, deliberately avoiding looking down through the floor at the inert, crumpled body below, and leant against the wall, gasping. There were tears in his eyes, but he did not know whether they were tears of sadness or anger, of frustration or relief. He was taking in great gulps of the acrid, smoky air, but they were filled with particles of ash and dirt, making him choke. The flames were now even closer than before, and their deep orange colour made them seem angrier than ever.

Then, somehow, through all of the chaos both within and without, Matthew and the others resurfaced in his mind, and this recollection enabled him to regain his senses. As his feeling of focus returned, Charles drew himself upright and wiped the grime from his face.

He had to get out of here.

And he had to reach the car.

But how?

To exit through the entrance hall would have been the

quickest route, but the explosion had ensured that this was no longer an option. He looked back at the corridor he had used to get here and saw that it was now engulfed in flame and was impassable. There were still two other passageways leading away from the foyer, but both had wisps of smoke drifting through them, so it was impossible to know which one was the safest. Charles selected one at random and began to run. As he did so, the portraits of stern-faced people long dead regarded him from their ornate frames, and suits of armour rattled as he passed by.

After a few moments of frantic running, Charles stopped and threw open the door to a little used side room. It was all in darkness, and the furniture was covered with dust sheets. Ignoring it all, he ran towards the window and, having pulled back the wooden shutters, began to wrestle with the window latch.

"And where do you think you're going?"

The blood froze in his veins. Charles slowly turned round to see the formidable and clearly enraged Mr Jolly, who was holding the baseball bat in one hand and the ugly, serrated dagger in the other. He was covered in sweat and grime, his arms and face were speckled with open lacerations and bruises, and his leather waistcoat hung from him in tatters.

The window was still closed.

Mr Jolly was blocking the door, and there was no other exit from the room.

Charles was trapped.

"Setting off all those explosives while we were still in there wasn't a very nice thing to do, now was it?"

The voice was deep and gravelly, and the words were uttered slowly and precisely. As he spoke, Mr Jolly tapped the bat against the side of his leather boot, slowly, and gave a mirthless smile. In the quietness of the room, the sound of wood on leather sounded decidedly sinister. The blade in the other hand was disturbingly long, as well as being finely honed and clearly razor sharp.

"Mr Garret was a good friend," Mr Jolly continued. "You might even say he was my only friend. You took him away from me." Mr Jolly was staring at Charles as he spoke, looking him straight in the eye, and his expression became impassive. "When your little gift went up, my friend caught the full force of the blast but I managed to get out just in time." As he spoke, his tone was quiet and almost casual. "I had to, you see, to make sure you got what you deserved."

Right at that moment, there was the sound of another explosion. Although it was some distance away, it was still ear-splitting.

"Ooh," said Mr Jolly, with mock seriousness, "what a dreadful noise. That sounded like a gas explosion to me. It seems that all those flames must've ruptured your pipes. I do hope you've got insurance."

He took a step towards Charles, who took an instinctive step backwards.

"Look," said Charles, trying to convey a feeling of confidence which he didn't feel at all, "the whole house is on fire, and the flames will reach us soon. If we don't get out now we'll both be burned to death."

"Is that supposed to frighten me?" asked Mr Jolly. "I've already cheated death once today, so I reckon Lady Luck is on my side. However, as I'm sure you will have realised by now, she is most definitely not on yours."

Barely had the words left his lips when Mr Jolly suddenly lunged towards Charles, wielding both the bat and the blade with evident dexterity, and moving with surprising swiftness for someone so portly. In just the nick of time, Charles managed to sidestep, dodging both of the swinging weapons as they whooshed through the air in deadly arcs, missing him by only the narrowest of margins.

Mr Jolly paused.

"Impressive," he said, displaying a sarcastic grin, and tapping the bat against the arm of a chair. "Usually, I catch my prey on the first attempt. I hope I'm not losing my touch."

He let out a yell, and charged again. By some miracle, at the last moment the nervous Charles ducked to one side. The momentum carried Mr Jolly past Charles and further into the room and, seeing his chance, Charles began to sprint for the door.

"I don't think so," growled Mr Jolly. With a practised flick of the wrist, he hurled the bat across the room. As it sped towards its victim, the expertly-thrown weapon was right on target, close to the floor and spinning like the rotor blades of a helicopter. Charles felt the impact of the bat as it became entangled in his legs. He lost his balance and fell, heavily.

"Do be careful," smirked Mr Jolly. "I wouldn't want you to hurt yourself. Far better to leave that to me."

Charles was already starting to scramble to his feet, but before he could do so he felt a brutal kick in his side. He groaned and collapsed again and, a moment later, he found himself lying with a heavy, booted foot thrust against his chest, pinning him to the floor.

"Leaving so soon?" asked Mr Jolly. "Surely not. The party is only just beginning."

He brandished the blade, and ran his thumb along its sharpened edge, nodding approvingly.

"Did I mention," he said, "that this blade is brand new? I haven't really had the chance to test it out yet."

Charles struggled and squirmed, but was unable to escape from beneath the weight of his hefty assailant as he bore down upon him. Mr Jolly pretended not to notice, but continued to speak, in the same casual manner.

"Whenever I use a blade for the first time," he said, looking closely at the weapon, "I can never make my mind up as to whether I should try a series of frenzied, rapid stabs, or whether I should just do one satisfyingly deep plunge and then give it a good twist." He paused and then regarded the writhing figure under his foot. "What do you think I should do?" he asked.

Charles could no longer hear the howling winds outside. Nor could he smell the smoke or hear the roar of the approaching flames. All he could see was that long, cruel blade, as it was held, glinting, high in the air.

"What? You have no answer?" said Mr Jolly. "I suppose it is quite a difficult choice. Hmm… in that case, perhaps I should compromise, and do both. Does that sound like a satisfactory solution?"

Charles writhed and thrashed, but he was held fast by sheer brute force of the leather boot which was planted firmly on his torso.

"All right then," said Mr Jolly. "It's time to do what I came for. Thanks for the chase. I enjoyed it."

His eyes narrowed and his expression hardened. He then let out a loud cry of triumph, and brought the blade down with a movement which was both fast and deadly

Charles screamed and closed his eyes, wrapping his arms around his head and face, in a futile attempt to defend himself.

At that same split second, another figure dashed into the room and shoulder-barged the attacker. Mr Jolly grunted as he was shoved off balance and stumbled, while the blade swung wide, missing its target by mere inches.

"Come on!" Matthew yelled, as he grabbed the trembling Charles and helped him to his feet.

The two of them ran out of the room and into the corridor. The flames had advanced further along the corridor, and the smoke was much thicker now, making it difficult to breathe. Through momentary gaps in the acrid mist, the raging inferno could be seen as it came nearer and nearer.

"Make for the window at the far end," said Matthew, "but we'll have to crawl. There's always a layer of clear air close to the floor."

That was true, up to a point; the air *was* clearer at floor level. Nevertheless, they both still found themselves inhaling flakes of hot ash, as they coughed and spluttered their way on hands and knees as fast as they could.

"Where are you?" screamed Mr Jolly, as he staggered from the room behind them. He had now recovered the baseball bat, and was waving it around to try and disperse some of the smoke. "You won't escape. I'll find you, wherever you are!"

Under the cover of the smoke, Charles and Matthew were hidden from the view of their crazed pursuer. They scurried along the floor and finally reached the end of the corridor.

"Stay down," said Matthew. "I'll try to get the window open."

He took a lungful of the unpleasant air. Then, steeling himself, he rose up into the smoke, groping in the gloom for the window latch. After just a few moments he found what he was searching for, but the blasted thing refused to budge.

"Hurry up!" cried Charles. "The flames are getting closer."

He immediately regretted shouting so loudly, since the flames weren't the only thing for them to worry about.

The unmistakeable sound of Mr Jolly's footsteps could be heard approaching too. Somehow, he seemed impervious to the smoke and was continuing to walk through it as normal.

"Come out, come out, wherever you are," he said, in a hoarse, guttural whisper, as he continued to wave the bat back and forth in the veil of smoke.

Summoning all his strength, and with his teeth gritted, Matthew twisted the latch and it finally came unstuck. Sliding his fingers under the frame he tried to lift it, but the window still remained steadfastly shut. With both the fire and Mr Jolly now very close indeed, a wave of desperation swept over Matthew, as he realised he needed to locate a second latch.

In just a few moments, he managed to find it, and was relieved to find that this one could be released much more easily. However, his relief was short-lived.

"Aww, ain't that a pity," said Mr Jolly, as he emerged from the acrid vapour. "So near and yet so far. Now, just leave that window alone, there's a good boy."

Despite the smoke, both the bat and the blade came into sharp focus in Charles' vision. There was nowhere left to run. Terrified, he pushed himself back against the wall, beneath the window.

"Don't worry," said Mr Jolly. "I promise this will all be over very soon. Now, which one of you would like to go first?"

Charles and Matthew stared back at him, saying nothing.

"What? No answer? Well, in that case, I hope you'll allow me to make the decision."

Mr Jolly lunged.

Charles closed his eyes.

At that moment, Matthew abruptly reached back and, grabbing the edge of the window, slid it fully open in a single, smooth motion. At the same instant, he threw himself flat on the floor, pulling Charles down with him. Outside, the high winds created a sudden inflow of oxygen which drew the flames towards the window with alarming rapidity. Spinning round, Mr Jolly had just enough time to see the approach of the oncoming fireball before he was completely engulfed by it. Screaming, he flailed around, with his clothing aflame.

Charles and Matthew kept their heads down as the flames roared above them, and out through the open window.

But Mr Jolly was not finished yet.

"I'm gonna take you with me," shrieked the crazed attacker.

With his clothes on fire, and ignoring the agony of his burning flesh, the walking inferno staggered towards the two men now cowering in the corner. He had dropped the baseball bat somewhere, but the knife was still firmly in his grasp. He drew nearer, and half a smile formed on what remained of the flaming apparition's lips. He raised the blade high.

Just then, a very loud and ominous cracking sound was heard. Glancing upward, Mr Jolly saw a flaming beam fall from the ceiling directly above him. He swiftly side-stepped, successfully avoiding the fiery timber as it came crashing to the floor, sending up a shower of sparks.

Mr Jolly laughed – he actually laughed – as he turned back to Charles and Matthew.

"Seems I was right about Lady Luck," he gloated. "Now, it's time to finish this, once and for all."

He took a step towards them, but then a second beam came down, and this time he was unable to avoid it. It fell directly on top of him, heavily, pinning his blazing form to the floor. He thrashed around, screaming, as the flames finally completed their grizzly work, but Charles and Matthew did not wait around to watch. The falling beams had given the flames something new to devour, causing them to move back from the window. Seeing their chance, Charles and Matthew heaved themselves out over the sill, and ignoring the maelstrom which still raged outside, they lost no time in running from the house as speedily as they could.

***

"Here! Over here, sir!" James called above the gale and waving, as he saw Charles and Matthew emerge from the burning building.

They heard, and headed in his direction. They were both covered in soot and grime, but appeared otherwise unharmed.

"I really am most relieved to see you," said James, "but just look at the dear old house. I asked Mrs Gillcarey to call the fire brigade, but I fear there is little they will be able to do at this stage."

The three of them turned to look, and it was a sorry sight indeed.

Whilst much of the stonework was still standing, the very larger part of the internal wooden structure had now vanished altogether, while the unrelenting flames continued to exert their destructive force on those parts which remained. This once proud, magnificent dwelling was now nothing more than a gutted shell, covered with a pall of thick, pungent smoke.

Matthew looked at Charles, and softly spoke a single word.

"Krsitin?" he asked.

Charles didn't reply, but shook his head.

"If possible," said Matthew, after a moment of pause, "we need to get to the car and drive to the Lodge, as planned. They'll be wondering what's happened to us."

"We must go carefully though, sir," said James. "I noticed the car was parked very close to the house."

A couple of minutes later, they reached the vehicle, which was waiting for them where they had left it, close to what remained of the front door, though it was now coated with a thick covering of ash.

In silence, they gazed up at what had once been an imposing façade, and James, fishing a handkerchief from his pocket, dabbed at his glazed eyes.

Then, from the house itself, came a sound unlike anything that any of them had ever heard before.

Lord Alfred Willoughby's 'surprise' had worked far more effectively than he could ever have imagined. The explosion in the dynamite room had not just ripped a hole through the entrance hall floor; it had also cracked the foundations of the building itself. The valiant structure had tried its best to remain erect as long as it could, but now the inevitable pull of gravity began to take its toll.

The high façade began to teeter. Rocking back and forth, slowly at first, but spurred on by the unrelenting wind, it quickly began to look very unsteady indeed.

"I suggest we retreat to a safe distance," said Matthew, making for the car and leaping into the driver's seat.

There were no dissenting voices, and the others joined him as rapidly as they could.

Barely had the keys been turned in the ignition when there was heard an almighty crash. Matthew sped the car to a safe distance away, then pulled to a halt. As the three occupants looked behind them, they could scarcely believe what they were seeing, and scrambled from the vehicle to witness the unbelievable sight.

Encircling Heston Grange, an enormous ring-shaped hole had opened up. Huge quantities of earth had simply fallen away, leaving the house itself balanced precariously on an island in the middle.

"The dear old girl doesn't have long now," whispered James.

How right he was.

Only moments later, the entire front of the grand old mansion, still burning fiercely, began to bend and flex. The howling wind, sensing its opportunity, now increased its ferocity. Then, with an ear-splitting squeal as bricks and mortar, and stone and steel began to separate, it became detached from the rest of the house; and then, almost in slow motion, it pitched forward into the abyss.

Through momentary gaps in the ensuing great cloud of billowing dust, many of the rooms within could now be glimpsed, along with their contents. However, all that furniture, together with all the fixtures and fittings, did not remain on display for long.

The floors of the newly revealed rooms slowly began to slope and distort, causing tables, chairs, beds, wardrobes and all manner of other charred and blackened household items to slide closer to the edge before finally toppling into the chasm and dropping into the depths of the earth beneath.

The expressions on the faces of Charles, Matthew and James were of utter disbelief, and the collapse of the rest of the house was now inevitable. Sure enough, now that the frontage had gone, within moments the remaining walls began to sag and sway. Powerless against the forces of nature and gravity, one by one, they all met the same fate. Only the octagonal tower still stood, looking decidedly isolated and lonely in the midst of the surrounding carnage and destruction, and with the broken remains of the rickety bridge hanging, limply, at its side, being blown about in the wind like a withered vine.

But even that was not the end of it.

The elements had one further card to play.

The combined force of the two mighty explosions had done more than just crack the foundations of the house. They had also caused ruptures within the nearby soft chalk cliffs. Colossal portions of the weakened rock had already fallen away. Now, the powerful waves of the ocean, having waited so long for this moment, and spurred on by the aggressive, angry winds, finally broke through, and the ground beneath the tower began to subside. Remarkably, the structure itself remained more or less intact as it slowly descended into the sinkhole, the final symbol of a period of history and a bygone era, still doing its best to stand strong, right up until the very end.

And then, at last, the winds ceased their violent assault, and a strange calm settled upon the surreal scene.

"That's something you don't see every day," Matthew breathed.

James merely grunted in agreement, while Charles had such a lump in his throat he found he could make no sound at all.

A lone seagull flew overhead, its plaintive screech adding a deeply poignant quality to the moment.

No one spoke for a long time.

Eventually, it was the loyal butler, James, who broke the silence.

"What will you do now, sir?" he asked.

Charles, who had yet to take his eyes from the scene of devastation before him, was jolted from his semi-trance by the question. He wiped away a couple of tears from his eyes before he answered.

"What? Oh, well, I expect I'll go up to the estate in Galloway. I'm not sure I have any other option, but I sincerely hope that you and Mrs Gillcarey will join me."

James smiled.

"Of course, I shall come with you," he said, "but as for Mrs Gillcarey, you must ask her yourself. Perhaps we should go to the Lodge now?"

"Yes, of course. I just need a moment longer."

Charles looked back towards the site of the once grand

property, with many memories coursing through his mind. He still couldn't quite believe what had happened.

The flames had gone now, though small plumes of smoke could still be seen, here and there.

After gazing at the scene for a while, Charles continued to look straight ahead as he asked, "And what about you, Matthew? What will you do?"

"Right now, I don't know," came the reply. "I suppose I'm open to ideas. I only came here in the first place because I was being pressurised by the Boss, but I decided early on that I was not going to let him get his grubby hands on the Willoughby fortune."

"I know, and I'm most grateful – though, as I told you, the fortune is nowhere near as large now as it used to be."

"When the Boss hears about what's happened," said Matthew, "he's not going to be pleased. He'll almost certainly send someone after me."

"But he can only do that if he knows where you are, right?"

"Well, yes, but –"

"Why don't you come to Galloway too? It's most unlikely this Boss character will find us up there. Heston Grange is now destroyed and his henchmen are dead. With a bit of luck he'll think that you went down with the ship as well."

Matthew gave a small smile and looked back to where his old home had stood.

"It was a great house, wasn't it?"

"Indeed it was, though I've known for some time that it would become uninhabitable eventually. As it turns out, it happened sooner than I would have liked, but life does play tricks on us sometimes."

"Indeed it does," said Matthew. "Indeed it does."

The exhausted trio returned to the car and began to drive towards the lodge.

A few moments later they pulled up outside but, before they had a chance to get out of the car, Meg came bustling out of the cottage towards them.

"James! There you are! Whatever took you so long?" she said. "Mrs Gillcarey has been here for ages already. Anyway, the kettle's on, and I have some of your favourite flapjacks ready. Your friends may come in too, if they want, so long as they wipe their feet."

She turned away and went back into the lodge.

Charles looked at Matthew and James.

"Tea and flapjacks sounds nice," he said. "Shall we?"

The flapjacks turned out to be Chelsea buns, but at least their cups of tea were hot this time.

The tiny sitting room of Heston Lodge was not really designed to seat five people, but no one commented as they squeezed themselves into the small pieces of furniture.

Occasionally, someone made some slight attempt at conversation. For the most part, though, they sipped and chewed in silence, thinking back over all the recent events, feeling grateful to have survived the ordeal, and remembering those who had not.

Meg spent the entire time simply staring at James and looking content.

***

Not far away, the surging waters which had broken through the chalk cliffs and finally brought down the iconic octagonal tower, now being propelled by the ocean swell, began to rise. Little by little, their natural ebb and flow increased, bringing the level within the sinkhole a little higher with each incoming surge; and, bit by bit, those portions of the tower which still remained visible above the surface began to diminish.

And, just a little further along, the very last pieces of the pillars and posts of the main house which were still standing gradually cracked and crumbled, one by one, and disappeared into the foam, as the waters finally closed over the fragments of Heston Grange.

EPILOGUE

It was taking too long.

He should have heard something by now.

The Boss sat in his cell, the fingers of his two enormous hands interlocked, as he rested the huge, gnarled fists on his desk.

Since he was expecting to hear something imminently, maybe he was just being over-eager, he kept trying to tell himself. Perhaps his associates just needed a little more time.

Yet his instinct told him differently.

Garret was a reliable man to have on side, and the fact that he had decided to take along Mr Jolly to assist with this particular project virtually guaranteed a successful outcome.

On the numerous occasions in the past when the Boss had engaged Garret's services, he had never been let down. This time, though, the more he thought about it, the stronger his suspicion became that something had gone seriously wrong.

But what could it be? What had happened?

He needed to find out.

If Garret had double-crossed him, the Boss had other avenues he could explore, and other contacts he could call upon, to help piece together whatever had taken place. Right now, however, the fact that his unusually valuable prize appeared to be in danger of slipping straight through his fat fingers was causing an intense consternation to rise within him.

In a rare moment of uncontrolled frustration, the Boss let out a scream and slammed his fists down hard onto the desk. A short distance away, along the metal gantry, a guard heard the outburst, but knew better than to approach the cell at the end of the corridor.

The Boss glanced up at the clock and considered. Down in the quadrangle, there were still a few minutes of exercise time remaining. If he was quick, he might have just enough time to get a message out via his friend, the sympathetic prison guard.

As he thought of this, his ugly features twisted into a self-satisfied smirk. It always amazed him to find how cheaply some supposedly upstanding men could be bought.

A look of resolve and determination appeared on his face. Swiftly, he reached for a sheet of paper. Then, picking up a pencil, he began to write.

Other books by Richard Storry

The Black Talisman

1673: Deep in a deserted forest, a coven of witches is taken by surprise as they attempt to summon the dark Lord, Anubin, from the spirit world.

1984: At his Easter camp, a young boy has an amazing divine encounter. However, as the subsequent years pass, he and his girlfriend find themselves increasingly the subject of demonic visitations.

What is the connection between these seemingly isolated events, over 300 years apart? As the angelic forces of good and evil clash, the mystery gradually emerges.

Can the dark servants of Anubin be prevented from obtaining for him the power he so fervently seeks — the power that comes from the black talisman?

The Cryptic Lines

Living as a recluse in his remote gothic mansion, the elderly Lord Willoughby knows that he does not have long to live. With little time remaining, he needs to decide what will become of his vast fortune after his death.

Not content to simply hand everything over to his wastrel son, Matthew, he decides, instead, to set a series of enigmatic puzzles which the son must solve if he is to inherit the estate. However, it emerges that Matthew is not the only interested party. The old house holds many secrets, and nothing is as it first appears....

Order of Merit

In *Order of Merit* we encounter a concert guitarist who is known and loved by audiences all over the world, not only because of his masterful technical skill and compelling musicality, but also because of his charismatic stage personality.

However, his consummate showmanship is merely a cover for his more sinister occupation.

Away from the spotlight he is also a professional hitman – cold, ruthless and efficient. Cunning and calculating, his missions are always accomplished fully, expertly and without a hitch.

But when his next target turns out to be a relative of one of his best friends, things can only get ugly.

The Virtual Lives of Godfrey Plunkett

To relieve his monotonous life of humdrum tedium, Godfrey Plunkett frequently escapes into the world of his fertile imagination. There, away from all criticism and the disparaging looks from his fellow human beings, he can be free to live his dreams. Here, he can be a hero, a celebrity, a movie star – anything he wants.

And, somehow, these inner thoughts help him to maintain his optimism that something fantastic is waiting for him, just around the corner, and is about to happen for real, at any moment.

But, out there in the harsh, real world, will anything fulfilling or exciting ever really happen for this poor, misunderstood individual? Or is he destined to only ever experience the excitement of life within the privacy of his own thoughts?

And, more importantly, what happens when the dividing line between reality and his make-believe world starts to blur?

Come and find out. Come and experience the virtual lives of Godfrey Plunkett.

Ruritanian Rogues, Volume I: A Looming of Vultures

While an ugly war with its neighbouring realm continues to rage, the insulated members of Ruritania's upper classes laugh and dance their way through their superficial lives. Some people, increasingly disillusioned by the pointless conflict, start to consider how the King might be persuaded – or forced – to end it. Meanwhile, an increasing number of items of great value are going missing from those attending these high society gatherings. At whom will the finger of suspicion point? Can anyone be trusted? Why is Captain Golovkin acting so strangely? And is Baron Rudolph really the darling of society he appears to be? In this swirling cauldron of agendas, what will emerge from this looming of vultures?

All titles are available from www.crypticpublications.com in paperback, in audio format and as downloads for e-readers.

You can also use this site to contact Richard directly, if you wish. He is always pleased to hear from readers, and will be happy to answer any questions about his books.

Printed in Great Britain
by Amazon

48718938R00137